Praise for *Parsimony*

"Peter Nash imbues each line of elegant prose with a pervasive sense of unease. Along with the unfolding drama of the Ansky family, *Parsimony* skillfully evokes the controversies of one American decade after another. I was startled again and again by the shock of recognition—and by the all too relevant warning: how easily we defend ourselves against seeing systems of cruelty when blinded by conviction and hope, or by their absence."
— Diane Lefer, author of *Confessions of a Carnivore* and *California Transit: Stories*

"Peter Nash's evocative exploration of the complex relationship between a son and his father possesses the melancholy wisdom of Philip Roth's *Patrimony*, the sense that we can never really know those closest to us until we know ourselves. Nash writes like a poet; his sentences unwind through ideas, emotions, and wise reflections on the sadness of aging, the difficulties of parenting, and the trials of sustaining intimacy when so much stands in the way. I loved this book for its quiet wisdom and for its commitment to telling the most daunting truths about growing apart from those with whom we share the most."
—George Ovitt, author of *The Snowman* and *What Happens Next*

Parsimony

PETER NASH

FOMITE
BURLINGTON, VT

This is a work of fiction. While some scenes in the novel were inspired by actual people and events, they have been used in a fictitious manner.

Cover art — Gespenst eines Genies, no. 10 [Ghost of a Genius] Paul Klee, Scottish National Gallery of Modern Art

ISBN-13: 978-1-944388-11-9
Library of Congress Control Number: 2017940164

07-30-2023

For Annie, Ezra, and Isaiah

In memory of Robert S. Starobin
(1939-1971)

Oh, it was blue, the too amenable sea.

We heard of pearls in the dark and wished to dive.

But here in this snail-shell see, see

The crab-legs waggle; where,

If altered now, and yet alive,

Did softness get these bitter claws to wear?

Richard Wilbur

ONE

IN THE PHOTOGRAPH I am nine, maybe ten years old. Only the tight, ammonitic spiral of the stairs on which I stand, glaring up at my mother's Instamatic, confirms the fact that they are Gaudí's stairs, that I was ever in his basilica at all. Now my mother is dead and Gaudí is dead and my father is looking at the television where he sits on his lanai in his skullcap and slippers with his back to the view my mother loved so well of the dying red mangroves, and of Sanibel Island, where she'd collected shells in the wintertime, some of the finest in the world, to mail to her friends who are themselves all dead now, puffs of phosphorous, dust.

It has been years since I've looked at this photo album, since my mother's last birthday at least, when my sister, Lily, giddy as a girl and fairly drunk on champagne, had passed the book around to prove to everyone that she'd once been blonde. I tried to reach her by telephone this morning, back in Ithaca where she's returned with her son to live, but she rarely answers my calls these days, knowing as she does what I'll say.

Yet I'll never repeat the words. She should know this about me, that I'll never cross the same bridge twice.

As a child Lily had trusted me, trusted everyone. She'd smiled and laughed and held the hands of the mumbling young supplicants who'd appeared at our door, hats in hand, to walk with our father in the glen behind the house. Then, people had sought him out, this son of Joseph Ansky, driving the five long hours from the city, eager—as often one is eager with the children of celebrities—to glimpse the parent beneath the skin. For, as much as my father had published in our years of living in Ithaca, as much as he'd distinguished himself in his own stubborn right (climbing the ladder we'd kept by the woodshed in my dreams until there were no more rungs to climb), he'd never been able to shake his father's long shadow, so that by the end of his career he'd been haunted by the impression that the old man was actually stalking him through the glens.

Still his father's shadow was nothing compared to his voice, that ardent, histrionic voice, the like of which one can only hear in old newsreels anymore, a voice so bold, so presumptuous, it used to suck the air from my lungs when he answered the battered red door of his apartment to let us in.

More than that, I can scarcely remember the man, my father's obloquial father. Before we left New York, he was still living in a poorly lit walk-up in Morningside Heights, just a half a dozen blocks from our building, though he might have been living in a different city altogether for the little we saw of him. It was only on the occasional Sunday that my father had bothered us to know him at all, inspecting our clothes and hair before marching us across Broadway, there at the university gates, then down the other side.

On those mornings we rarely spoke, filing past the

empty shops and restaurants with their heavy, padlocked grilles, and crossing at the intersections without waiting for the lights. For it was usually early when we started out, the streets cold and steaming, my father striding ahead of us in silent communion with himself, only to turn upon our dawdling some days with an anger, an impatience, that seemed to speak of other things.

I'd liked the city at that hour when people were just beginning to stir, raising the shades on their windows and peering expectantly into the streets. Now and then we'd crossed paths with some other early riser, some old woman with a dog or a homeless man pushing his cart of bottles and cans, but such encounters were rare.

It was in the course of those early morning treks that my father had seemed to shrink in size, retreating within himself, like in a turtle in its shell—back humped, head and hands drawn deep inside his coat. He'd walked swiftly, expelling great white puffs of cigarette smoke through which my sister and I had had to scurry to catch up to him, only to lose pace with him again by the end of the next block.

It had been my father's custom to stop once along the way, at the same bodega, for coffee, bread, and cigarettes, which he'd had me present to his father with a curt if gracious bow. I'd never liked the scruffy old man—his thick, moist lips, the dark bags beneath his eyes—and remember the fear I'd felt each time we'd climbed the narrow stairs in his building, remember hating the way he'd smelled.

Lily herself was never fazed by him; she'd chattered away at the bearded old atheist like a little magpie, rooting through his deep woolen pockets for candy and change, and helping herself to the Danish biscuits in the tin beneath the sink. And she'd thought nothing, each time we'd visited our grandfather, of making herself at home in his cramped, Cimmerian study with its 'squirrel's-eye' view of St. John the Unfinished (as he'd dubbed the cathedral across the street), pushing aside his books and journals and outdated stacks of the *Daily Worker* to make a place for herself where she'd drawn her little pictures of rainbows and castles, which she'd pinned without permission to the shelf above his desk. She'd never minded the view, so grimly medieval, never noticed the soaring fretwork of silver tubes and planking over which the masons had scrambled like spiders each day in their race against our grandfather, with all his Marx and manifestos, for the very soul of Humankind.

He'd had a window in the kitchen where I used to sit beside the radiator as he and my father smoked cigarettes and talked. Through the dingy lace curtains, which had always suggested the hand of a woman, a wife, I'd looked out upon the avenue, upon the cathedral and park, and upon the steady stream of customers—students largely—passing in and out of the Hungarian coffee shop below. Mostly they'd argued, my father and grandfather, scraping their chairs and whispering through their teeth. They'd argued about welfare and taxes, and about the war in Vietnam, about Johnson, the Tet Offensive, and the Gulf of Tonkin, which I'd always pictured as beautiful and blue and speckled with Chinese junks. They'd seemed to disagree about everything, about the unions and Mayor Lindsay, about the drawbridges on the Harlem River, about the heaps of garbage in the streets, clashing even over the university's plan—so innocuous to me—to build a gymnasium in Morningside Park. Each time they'd met they'd argued with such vehemence, such gall, that on one occasion my sister had burst into tears, refusing to be comforted until my grandfather took her up to see the pigeons on the roof.

But Lily trusts no one now, least of all me. No inducement on my part could persuade her to join me here in Florida, to help me with our father who changes shape before my eyes, flitting nimbly between moods, sensing, dreading as he does, the reason I am here, and hoping that if only he ignores me I will take up my suitcase and go.

This time I brought my daughter Rachael with me in the feckless expectation that she would help to fill the space between my father and me, while I organized his papers and sorted his things, but since we arrived yesterday she has barely moved from the lounge chair by the pool downstairs, rousing herself only long enough to apply more lotion to her still-skinny arms and legs. She has never really known my father; there has never been the expectation that she should, that she should care about this mawkish old man who sits slumped before the television and can't remember her name.

He has let the apartment go, my father, his daily circuit reduced to a single, wobbly loop between the bathroom and his chair on the lanai where he dozes fitfully beneath a potted palm amidst his prayer books and pills, conjuring troupes of old antagonists who cluster round him in their motley to moot and bandy with him over the blare of the television until he drives them from the room with a fist. Then he is calm again, smiling, sighing, when he speaks of my mother and cries.

This morning I told him that the charges had been dropped, but he pretended not to hear me, to care, averting his eyes and raising the volume on the set to prevent me from telling him the rest. For he knows what this means.

This time he actually struck the maid, then tried to strangle her before she escaped out the door, a report confirmed by one Sergeant Salinas of the local police department who'd been kind enough, at the time, to work with me over the telephone where I was consulting on a job near Chengdu, so that it has been at least a couple of weeks since my father's apartment was cleaned, since the bedrooms were tidied, the sinks and toilets scrubbed.

One of the first things I did upon our arrival yesterday was to raise the blinds and throw open the windows to dispel the fetid air, a simple, natural impulse that so angered my father that he fell from his chair, trembling like an epileptic until my daughter began to sing. —Such an odd and knowing reaction for a girl so young, for at once his face unclenched itself and his trembling ceased, so that together we were able to ease him back into his chair, when he looked at her, my Rachael, as though her lips were the petals of a wild pink rose.

Since yesterday he's spent most of the time mumbling and muttering to himself, a shambling colloquy with the air about him, broken only now and then by spells of catatonic stillness in which his face is washed clean of feeling and even his eyes shed their light, the remaining hairs on his head stirred gently by the warm gulf breeze. It is then that I approach him, that I examine him like a father a sleeping child; for then he is insensible to me, to my presence in the room. I can close the book in his lap and turn down the volume on the television; I can wipe his lips, trace the scar on his chest; and I can clip his cracked and yellowed nails, marveling, where I crouch beside his chair, at the oddly autonomous weight of his slender hands and feet. Removing his dirty glasses, I can look directly into his eyes—and all with an impunity unimaginable just a few months ago. For his decline has been swift, rising up out of the blue like one of the great tropical storms that batter this coast each year, toppling palm trees and power lines, ravaging the mangroves, and churning up the water so that for days the gulf looks brown. But then he snarls and spits; he fumbles for his glasses and I am forced to retreat to my place at the kitchen counter from where I watch him with a morbid fascination as he struggles with the objects in his lap, struggles to recognize and relate them—the prayer books, his cigarettes, the large-format remote control, grumbling, adjusting his shabby robe, then raising the volume on the set.

RACHAEL AND I HAD BEEN in the apartment for a good three hours yesterday before he even greeted me, stealing up behind me, where I sat busy in the kitchen, as if to foil a thief, only to lay a dry, speckled hand on my arm. For there are moments when he seems lucid, when he laughs at something on the television, when he seems to see me, his son, in all my incarnations at once, adding me up so quickly with his cold blue eyes I actually fear what he'll say.

Yet he has little to say about me—to me, that is. Instead he talks about chess, about the game on the board beside him (Tal-Lisitsin, Leningrad, 1956), and about the Yankees, about RBIs and ERAs, slapping at the local paper with the back of his hand (as I drift about the room behind him, admiring my mother's shells, her whelks and wentletraps and pearly white jingles, some as fine, as tiny, as the nail of a baby's toe) to express his disagreement with some sportswriter or other and swearing aloud to me that one of these days he'd give the mewling little bastard a piece of his mind.

It is in speaking of my mother that he is most familiar to me. Then his eyes light up, then he speaks with a clarity and affection that makes me think that little in him has changed.

Just this morning he'd surprised me with the story of the time my mother had found him—rescued him—after he'd broken his hip.

"It was snowing, it had been snowing hard all day," he'd told me, accepting the cup of instant coffee I'd made for him, only to set it aside. "I shouldn't have tried to fix the damned gutter. Your mother was right. Your mother had told me to wait until spring, until it was warmer, until the snow and ice were gone, but did I listen? No, of course not. Instead I put on my coat and hat, I got the ladder from the shed, and soon I was wiring up the gutter, though by then it was snowing so hard I could barely see my hands!" he'd explained to me with a chuckle, his eyes alert, his voice suddenly so composed, so sentient, I'd actually started at the change. "You know me, I've never let sense get in my way, so that there I was at the top of the ladder in the middle of a blizzard, one of the biggest in years, my fingers stiff, my face so numb I could hardly blink, when suddenly—my foot must have slipped—I was flat on my back on the ground, hip broken, howling in pain.

"I would have frozen to death had your mother not returned early from work that day," he'd added gravely, staring for a moment at the darkened television screen, when with a wistful smile he'd said, "You remember how it had snowed there, in Ithaca, how some winters it had fallen for days on end, how the lake itself had vanished, how the houses around us had simply disappeared, so that it had felt like we were living in some great white forest alone…

"That was how it was that year, the winter I broke my hip. It had snowed for more than a week without stopping, so that the ambulance had barely made it through…" he'd told me, fumbling for a cigarette, when briefly he'd hesitated, as though he'd lost his train of thought, only to recover with a snort, "Damned hospital! What a racket. You should have seen the bills! All those grinning doctors. Nothing but whipworms and vultures. Hell, if it wasn't for your mother, I'd have died there, would have perished where I fell. It happens fast, you know—the shivering, the numbness, the desperate craving for sleep…"

He'd had trouble lighting his cigarette, flicking the tiny wheel of his disposable lighter in vain until I'd found some matches for him, when upon a couple of fulsome puffs he'd continued, his voice strangely soft, discreet. "I remember the pain, yes. And I remember feeling drowsy. I remember just looking up at the snow tumbling down out of the pale gray sky and thinking random, silly things, like where was that green suit I used to wear, should I plant potatoes this spring, did your mother, your blessed mother, would she remember to pick up some gin? And I remember thinking that my shoes were too tight," he'd added vaguely, as if to himself, gazing absently about the room, only to take up one of the books from the table at his side, a brown-covered prayer book, which he'd raised to his nose to sniff.

The praying is something new. Last time I was here, the week after my marriage was annulled, he'd told me he'd been attending a local shul with a friend of his, a Lubavitcher shul in an old storefront by the Walmart near the highway. He'd told me it was bunk. Now he prays every day. No pork or shellfish. No dairy with meat. And he sings! For the first time in years I heard him singing this morning, just a humming really, as he prayed, a sound so full of feeling, so boyishly clear, I could only marvel at the grizzled old man where he sat nodding in his chair.

He'd never spoken of religion when we were children but with the greatest effort, snorting mulishly and working his heavy jaw as if forced to explain the principle of addition to a mentally retarded child. To speak of God was a kind of blasphemy in our house, a prohibition so strictly observed that my sister Lily had had to seek out the little Irish Catholic girl in the clapboard house next door for the chance to see the Mysteries for herself, sneaking hand-in-hand to nearby Immaculate Conception with the red-haired Claire McCaffrey and her devoted Auntie Peg, a bony spinster with crooked teeth who'd accidently betrayed her one day, while in conversation with my father, so that for more than a week he'd looked straight through my sister, refusing to acknowledge her existence even when she'd stamped her feet and cried. It was something he'd done to me on the occasions when I'd displeased him, so that it had taken me hours, sometimes days, to make myself real to him again, when he'd slip me a quarter or pat me on the head.

When I was twelve and my sister ten, my father had accepted a tenured position teaching Russian History at Cornell University in the Finger Lakes town of Ithaca, New York, an offer he'd accepted with alacrity, sick as he was of Manhattan and eager for a change. For years he'd bickered with his Columbia colleagues and had been happy, finally, to show them his back. He'd hated them all, often satirizing their books, which he'd kept for the purpose on a special shelf in his den, reading passages aloud to my mother over cocktails at night and mocking their turgid inscriptions to him. The day we left New York, he'd made a ceremony of discarding the books, dropping them one by one down the chute at the end of the hall.

I myself had dreaded the prospect of leaving New York, of leaving it again, for we'd only just returned to the city that May, after a fitful year of living in Mexico where my father had taken us to finish his book on Trotsky. As much as I'd liked the strange, unwonted country, the loose disorderly days in which so little had been expected of me, I'd been happy to be back in New York where I'd known that soon my father would be hard at work again at his teaching and research. I'd preferred him when he was tired at night, when he got home late, pulled off his tie, poured himself a bourbon, then sat to listen to his music in the den. If his day had not been bad, he might kiss my mother, tickle my sister, watch a little baseball with me. Since we'd returned to New York he'd seemed more at peace with the world, restored to himself by the familiar routine, as though the last of his demons had fled. That summer he and my mother had fallen in love again, taking walks along the river after dinner and spending Sunday mornings with the papers in bed.

The day he'd received the offer from Cornell he'd taken my mother to a restaurant to tell her the news. And it was then that the fighting had begun, begun anew, that everything between them had changed. I remember my father pleading with my mother and my mother refusing to open the bedroom door. For what had seemed like weeks they'd eyed each other as strangers, speaking only when forced to and eating their meals apart.

Then one day my mother simply had acquiesced, as if too tired to fight him anymore, though it was plain she'd resented him for uprooting us again. Clearly she'd rued the idea of leaving her many friends and associates in New York, and of surrendering our large university apartment, with its wide river view, comforting my sister and me, as best she was able, and dutifully packing our things.

For the first six months we'd rented a dismal, grayish-white frame house on East Seneca Street, the house in which the writer Nabokov had lived while teaching at Cornell, and I remember how endless the winter had seemed, the sky hard and gray, the trees glazed with ice, the cold wind whipping off the lake and penetrating every crack around the warped and misfit windows, so that there was little we could do to keep warm.

And I remember its particular scent, that first winter on the hill—a soporific, vaguely disquieting mixture of wood smoke, turpentine, and rotted leaves that even now, if I concentrate, has the power to make me drowsy.

I'd never seen my father so happy as in our first year of living in Ithaca. Never a very sociable man, he'd fraternized regularly with his university colleagues, hiked the paths along Fall Creek between classes in his sturdy boots and green felt hat, and generally praised the students there as some of the best and brightest he'd known.

That spring he'd surprised us with the news that he'd found a house for us at last, a large Italianate Victorian perched high above the lake on one of the steep hanging deltas near the university. For years a small hotel, the place had stood empty for nearly a decade when my father closed the deal on it, so that it had come as a disappointment to my sister and me when we first beheld it at the end of the shady, elm-lined street—the broken windows, the sagging porches, the high square cupola in which some pigeons had made their home.

The proprietress, a widow named Grote, had jumped to her death one very cold winter from one of the footbridges over Cascadilla Gorge, which gorge I could see from my bedroom window once the trees shed their leaves, so that I often thought of her as I sat in my room or wandered the high-walled garden out back, with its bacchanalian urns and putti statues and naked espaliers. For her spirit still lingered there, long after her death: I could sense it in the winding brick paths, some of which ended blindly at a tree or wall; in the all-but-natural-seeming disposition of the rocks; and in the shape of certain branches, so tenderly, gracefully pruned.

And she'd left her mark inside the house as well: above the wainscoting in the kitchen she'd painted a delicate floral border to match the pattern on the three stools and bread-box that her neighbor had made her as a gift.

I'd learned this from her neighbor himself, a Mr. Rabi-novich, who'd surprised me one day, shortly after we'd taken possession of the house, when I'd found him standing shirt-less in the garden where I'd gone to look for worms. He'd come to check the pump, he'd told me simply, with nei-ther handshake nor smile, getting down on his knees with a series of grunts and exclamations to examine the little pump at the base of the tall white fountain of Rebecca at the Well. And it was then that it had all come clear to me, that I'd understood that it was he who had diligently maintained the garden all those years, as the house itself fell to ruin. It was he, Mr. Rabinovich, who had clipped the grass and swept the walkways and kept the birdbaths filled, he, Mr. Rabi-novich, who had pruned the roses and scrubbed the foun-tain clean. Quite by chance I had solved the little mystery that had so baffled us all. Mr. Rabinovich had been in love with the widow Grote, I'd realized that day with a sudden expansiveness that had made me dizzy where I stood. He'd come to the garden each day to mourn her in the only way he'd known how, so that all I could think of as he'd knelt before me at the fountain that day was that he was kneeling at her grave. And so it had seemed to me each time he'd appeared in the yard to rake the grass or trim the honey-suckle or adjust the hinges on the crooked old gate.

Mr. Rabinovich had lived in Ithaca since the '40's, I'd learned in time, born of a family of poor White Russian Jews, most of whom had been murdered by the Bolsheviks and were no longer familiar by name. As Jews they'd had to cast their lots, he'd explained to me one day, prying a carious brick from the pathway to get at the tree root beneath it. They'd had to cast their lots and had not cast well.

Of course I'd understood little of what he'd told me at the time, alert only to the peculiar tenor of his voice, whenever he'd spoken of his family (of which he was then the sole known survivor), its otherwise rusty timbre colored now and then by an odd vibration, an adumbration really, a shadow of sound, of sorrow, so faint I'd had to strain my ears to catch it.

Yet Mr. Rabinovich had been anything but glum. After years of travelling the world, he'd finally found his peace there in Ithaca, in the gorges and glens for which it is known. He'd told me as much himself, not long after we'd met, listing for me, with a realtor's magniloquence, the town's many and inestimable features, only to regale me, in the weeks and months that followed, with a generous sampling of his favorite local lore, rousing tales of petty gangsters, lovers' suicides, and wailing midnight ghosts.

In his many years of living in Ithaca, he'd made a hobby of drafting simple sketches of its most distinguished buildings and trees—the Masonic Temple, State Theater, and Clinton Hall; the white oaks, striped maples, and shagbark hickories—and making crabbed black notes in a small black journal he'd kept for the purpose in his oilskin vest. With no regard for chronology, and with the occasional prompting from his journal itself, licking a finger to turn the wrinkled pages, he'd told me about the once-thriving Tutelo Indian village of Coreorgonel, destroyed by Washington's troops in his war against the Iroquois, and about Ithaca's largely unsung role in the Underground Railroad, even taking me into his house one day to show me the cupboard behind which a half a dozen runaway slaves had once been ingeniously, luxuriously, concealed.

Such was the illusion of Ithaca, he'd insisted to me, on more than one occasion, the town I knew, the town I saw with my eyes each day, but a fraction of some larger, more numinous whole. "Take the lake down there," he'd remarked to me one day, directing my attention to the wintry sliver of gray through the trees. Did I know that there were caverns deep beneath it, a dazzling netherworld of tunnels and chambers more than 18,000 acres in size? Of course I'd had no idea, had never even heard of the Lansing salt mine in which he'd served as foreman for nearly twenty years, though I remember the delight I'd expressed at the thought of that ghastly, Stygian realm. It was a reaction, however innocent, that had only angered the man, furrowing his normally placid brow.

"No, no!" he'd exclaimed, swatting the air with impatience, only to cock his head at me, as if appraising me anew. "It's nothing like that, no, nothing dreadful at all." And there he'd faltered, so that for a moment his lips had quivered mutely where he'd stood. "It's like…it's like nothing you could know," he'd stammered at last. "The darkness, the light…the deep thrumming silence down there—so ancient, so lonely, it sits upon your chest like a billion tons of rock. And then there's the air," he'd whispered, amazed, snuffling abruptly through his thick, bullish nostrils, "like a baby just born—that greedy, gobbling breath…"

In our frequent encounters he'd often talked that way, circling round some mysterious core, which he'd never seemed willing or able to name. It was only in speaking about salt that he'd really ever been plain with me, talking often and at length about the different ways it had been mined and harvested throughout history, and sharing with me the details of his own experience as a young man working the Algarve flats of Portugal with the hardy paludiers. Eyes ablaze, he'd told me of Mahatma Gandhi and his march to the sea, of the fate of Lot's wife, of how from the single word 'sal' came the words salary and sausage and sauce. And I remember him boasting to me one day, opening his bass-like mouth for me to see, that his tongue had absorbed so much of the stuff in his years of working underground that he no longer had to season his food.

He'd talked of many such things on the occasions when I'd joined him in the yard, describing for me with his indiscriminate pleasure everything from the elaborate plumbing of the old water-cure hospitals, the rusted remains of which still encumbered the nearby hills like the fleshless vertebrae of some ancient hydrological beasts; to the mysterious 'mist-pouffers' or phantom thunderclaps that occurred on clear blue days, rattling plates and knocking pictures from the walls; to the work of the famed Harvard naturalist and glaciologist, Louis Agassiz Fuentes, who'd put the town of Ithaca on the ornithological map one day with his discovery, in the Cayuga Lake basin, of the Yellow-Bellied Sapsucker.

Mr. Rabinovich could be funny, too; with a chuckling he'd once shared with me, as we'd scoured the rocks behind his house for fossils, tapping here and there with our pick point hammers, the tale of the great rhinoceros hoax, a collegiate prank in which for days the people of the town had been made to believe—thanks to the footprints by the water's edge—that a rhino had drowned in the lake. And over time he'd sketched for me in my mind a map of the many cataracts and plunge pools he'd come to know so well, though he hadn't set foot in the glens in years.

He'd been an avid fossil collector, his defunct and dusky kitchen given over, by the time I met him, to the careless storage of his finds: his brachiopods, bivalves, and corals; his trilobites, cephalopods, and turtle-shell concretions. I'd fancied a particular fossil of his, a perfect pink ammonite he'd found while hunting the Great Basin Desert in Nevada one winter and strung upon a chain as a gift for a woman or girl, so that I'd been surprised then abashed one day when, long after I'd forgotten the fossil, he'd told me I could have it, lifting it off the nail by the sink and handing it to me as if freeing himself of some long-borne burden at last.

He'd shown me how to change the blades on the lawn-mower, how to divide the irises, and how, with a piece of wire and a little vinegar, to remove the mineral deposits from the fountain pump filter. Then one day my mother had found him slumped behind the wheel of his truck in his garage. At first, not knowing what I knew, she'd told me he'd gone to see some relatives. Then she'd told me he was sick, finally taking me out to lunch one day, some many months later, to tell me he was dead.

It was about that time that I first met Michael Radetsky, a handsome, bearded young man with curly black hair who'd just been hired at the university, thanks in part to my father's advocacy, as an associate professor in American History. The son of one of my father's colleagues from his days in Wisconsin, Michael was a radical young historian who'd cut his teeth at Berkeley, first as a member of SNCC and then as a leader in the Free Speech Movement, and was eager now to jump into the fray. For the country that year was wracked with discontent. The war in Vietnam was on its bloody last legs and universities from coast to coast were being rocked by protests in which cars were smashed, students beaten, and buildings set aflame.

Cornell, by contrast, had been strangely calm at the time, an oasis in the storm, or so it had seemed to me as I'd wandered the shady campus above the lake or accompanied my mother to the library where she'd sat to do her work. What I hadn't known then was that in April of '69, just months before our arrival in Ithaca, the student union, where I'd often sat with my mother over French fries and Cokes, had been occupied at the start of Parents' Weekend by eighty heavily armed members of the university's Afro-American Society in a standoff with the National Guard and local police that had lasted more than thirty-six hours. It was Michael himself who had told me of that, on one of his many evenings in our home. It was one of the reasons he'd agreed to teach at Cornell, sensing as he had that there was more unrest to come.

But such things had meant little to me then. I was far more interested in Michael's motorcycle (on the back of which, with my mother's permission, he'd often taken me for rides through the hills, to Geneva and Horseheads and Seneca Falls) and in his favorite records (those of Stanley

Turrentine, Miles Davis, and Thelonius Monk), which he'd discoursed upon at length to me when we'd listened to them together from the ratty wicker chairs on his porch.

He'd had some funny notions, too, a couple of which I remember to this day—that jazz was best listened to through an open window, that while white people could produce a thousand Rockefellers they could never make a single John Coltrane.

As a boy, I'd admired the loose and easy way that Michael had carried himself on the weekends in his patched-up jeans, crude leather sandals, and Indian-style headbands, smiling and bobbing his curly head as he walked as if in silent benediction to the world around him. I knew that he was popular with the students there, men and women alike, who were often to be found camped out at his house, listening to music, talking politics, and painting placards for one of the many rallies and sit-ins that sprang up around the campus that year.

Unwilling to settle in the faculty ghetto by the university, he'd bought a small farmhouse outside of town on the edge of a field near Etna with an eye toward growing his own vegetables and keeping some goats, repairing the sharply sloped roof and replacing the glass in the dog-house windows upstairs, from the pair of which I'd often gazed out across the fallow fields to a distant stand of trees.

To reach the loft—for it was little more than that—one had climbed a flight of stairs pitched steeply as the roof itself, and it was there that Michael had made his study, fitting out the roughly timbered space with a desk, a chair, and a single long shelf for his books. It was there, too (where I'd often sat listening to his strange dictations as my mother clattered away on his typewriter beneath a poster of Malcolm X), where in time he'd amass his secret arsenal of shotguns, hand grenades, and high-powered rifles, with one of which, a bolt-action Ruger, he would blow out his brains.

THERE IT IS, THAT SOUND. Stiff in his chair, he cocks his head and listens. Tink-swoosh. Tink-swoosh. It reminds him of the high, fine clink of a jeweler's hammer: then the terrible rushing of blood. Tink-swoosh. Tink-swoosh.

I'VE PREPARED FOR MY FATHER a bowl of the muesli he likes, though now that I've set it beside him he has no interest in it, roughly pushing it away so that it topples to the floor. To my knowledge he's eaten nothing since we arrived yesterday. But for a box of baking soda and some old lasagna that one of his neighbors must have left for him, the refrigerator is empty. The cabinets, too, are bare of all but the most impractical provisions: an unopened sack of flour, a bottle of vanilla extract, and an economy sized container of dried bay leaves.

Before flying down from New York I'd spoken with a woman at the company with which I'd contracted to deliver my father's meals each day, only to discover that he'd terminated the plan some months ago, refusing, as he'd subsequently explained to me, to even sniff their noxious treyf. Instead he'd chosen to have his meals delivered to him by the local chapter of Chabad, basic kosher meals, which, while tasteless, had the virtue, he'd insisted, of at least being clean.

Yesterday I met the rabbi himself, a pale, soft-spoken man

with the crepuscular habit of blinking his large, unwhole-some eyes. To my surprise he'd assumed no rights to my father, uncovering the simple meal for him and adjusting the pillows behind his back with the quiet confidence of a professional nurse before wiping my father's chin. When at the door I'd informed him that his services would no longer be required, he'd simply nodded his head and smiled.

I remember once seeing a photograph of my father as a teenager standing arm in arm between two bearded old Jews at the Western Wall, a few renegade sprigs of green drooping from the crack above his head. It had been taken during a visit he'd made to Jerusalem in the year he'd lived on a kibbutz in the Upper Galilee. Hair tousled beneath the requisite paper kippah, skin burnished by the sun, he'd looked virile, happy to be standing there in the blazing light between the grinning Hasidim with their shtreimels and peyes and black gabardine. Long lost now, the photo has survived as a puzzle in my mind, as I can't help wondering where it was I ever saw it in the first place, for, while my mother had no recollection of it when I pressed her on the matter some years before she died, my father claims never to have visited Jerusalem at all.

Still I am certain the photograph was real, not a figment of my imagination, as at times I've been forced to suppose, confident that at least once I saw it for myself, even held it in my hand. What I imagine is this, that my godless young father had agreed to pose there between the jolly Hasidim at the prodding of his fellow kibbutznik with the camera, intending it as a lark, a gag, perhaps planning to send the photo home to his father in the hope of getting a rise out of him. Who knows? For I can only guess at the facts, as my father has never spoken to me of that year he spent in Israel as a young man, that is except once to tell me the inscrutable story (triggered by what feeling I cannot say) of the old Arab in Nablus who'd stolen his shoes.

Growing up in Ithaca, my family had been unlike the other families I'd known from school—the Irish, the Poles, the Slovaks, the Greeks, all of whom had carried themselves, when dressed in their faiths, with a puzzling mixture of subjection and conceit. Jewish though we were, it was never something we'd spoken about, let alone celebrated. But for the curious way it had bound us to New York—to Brooklyn, Manhattan, and Queens—being Jewish signified nothing to my family at all. There were no holiday parties, no holiday foods, and no holiday songs. There were no rituals to recognize the weeks, the seasons, the years, no heirlooms to decorate our sideboards and shelves, no portraits above the mantel by which to commemorate our dead. Not even the Holocaust, in which so many Anskys and Kulbaks had perished, had been enough to rouse us to words—Jewish words, that is.

Yet it was hardly a matter of indifference. My father, like his father, hated fascism with a virulence bordering on obsession, his library at the back of our house in Ithaca a veritable archive of books and journals detailing every Nazi speech, directive, pamphlet, map, letter, roster, flyer, essay, memo, lecture, telegram, handbook, blueprint, textbook, cartoon, poster, magazine, film clip, and photo ever salvaged from the war.

It was there at the desk in my father's study, piled high

with academic journals and foreign newspapers, that I'd first learned about Hitler, Himmler, Goebbels, and Hess, that I'd discovered among the countless photographs from the war the stirring, now iconic image from the destruction of the Warsaw Ghetto of five Jews (their actual names—Hanka and Matylda Lemet Goldfinger, Leo Kartuzinsky, Golda Stavarowski, and Tsvi Nussbaum, the boy with upraised arms—then superimposed upon the print) as they were herded to their deaths by German soldiers, one of whom, the dreaded SS-Rottenführer, Josef Blösche, was also identified by name.

And it was there in my father's study, in one of the books by the chair in which he'd liked to listen to his Heifetz at night, that I'd learned the story of how at Treblinka the Nazis, in the way that a butcher might stroke a steer's muzzle before slitting its throat, had been so determined to keep the Jews calm until the moment of their destruction that at the end of the train line, just before the smoking crematoria, they'd erected the façade of a turn-of-the-century German station, complete with luggage carts, multidirectional signposts, and a handsome wooden clock on the bold white face of which—so these Jews and Gypsies must have realized with a gasp—the large Gothic hands had been fashioned in paint.

There was just one synagogue in Ithaca at the time, a Conservative congregation on Tioga Street called Temple Beth-El, and I remember some of the families that used to belong there, university families mostly—the Chernows, the Spiegelmans, the Loebs. I remember the way they'd emerged from the stolid brick building after the New Year's services, chattering away in their handsome city clothes, the boys in their colored yarmulkes and clip-on ties breaking for freedom the instant they'd reached the steps. Only the portrait of my father's bearded uncle Moise, which had hung on the wall behind the door in the den, had linked me directly to this remote, somehow ignominious past.

I knew that growing up my father had worshipped his father's younger brother, that as a teenager he'd spent his summers helping him out in his watch repair shop in Brownsville, Brooklyn and accompanying him to daily services at a nearby shul, a fact that had eventually caused a rift between the brothers, ending only after years of silence when Moise was struck dead by a bus one day while crossing Flatbush Avenue.

Of all his relatives my father had only ever spoken to me about Moise. As a boy he'd been fascinated by his uncle's piety and by his work (the two forever linked in his mind), by the clocks and watches that cluttered the gloomy little shop on Caton Avenue where he'd sat for hours at the chipped old banker's desk by the window in the back, marveling at the heaps of tiny spare parts: the hairsprings, winding stems, clutch wheels, and escapements, which had always brought to mind for him the abandoned machinery of some elfin factory of Time.

For my wedding he'd given me the watch his uncle had given him, the watch I'm wearing now, a triply signed 1940's Lemania chronograph that his uncle had purchased from the widow of a man, a British soldier killed at Suez. For weeks it has been losing time, some matter of minutes each day, a trivial concern that vexes me nonetheless, alert as I've become to its queer if dogged ticking.

By the clock on the stove it is nearly noon and I haven't given a thought to lunch, to whether or not Rachael is even hungry, though she eats so little anymore it's likely she'd decline any suggestion I made. She hadn't wanted to eat in the apartment last night, not liking the smell of it, so I'd taken her to an Italian restaurant by the marina where she'd only nibbled at the pizza.

At her suggestion we'd wandered out along the dock after dinner to watch the manatees grazing placidly on the seagrass in the brackish water there, and had soon found ourselves enchanted by the great ungainly beasts, by their large, lumpish bodies, by their wrinkled, primigenial faces that broke the surface here and there behind a screen of tiny bubbles.

She'd told me that she'd recently done a report on the hippopotamus for her science teacher, Mr. Chakarian, a handsome, irreverent young man whom I'd met on Parents' Night in September.

Since then she has often spoken of him, her teacher, extolling his intelligence, his wit, and quoting him at length in a voice so righteous, so charged with feeling, I can only envy her such faith. For faith it is. Or love. The crush of a teenage girl.

Recently, over dinner at her favorite Chinese restaurant, she'd boasted to me of Mr. Chakarian's heresy as a teacher at St. Clare's—of his belief in evolution and global warming, of the hushed, pin-dropping day when he'd removed the crucifix from above his classroom door.

"Mr. Chakarian said it was one of the best reports he'd ever read," she'd told me last night, moved more by the glow of this teacher's praise than by any expectation of mine.

"That's great," I'd replied. "I'm proud of you. He sounds like a pretty special guy."

"Yes, he is. And all the girls think so," she'd been quick to add, as if suddenly embarrassed by her zeal. "You know he lived in Africa, in Botswana for a while, working for the Peace Corps. He says that the classroom is nothing compared to a day in the bush."

I'd said nothing, not wishing to deter her, only gazed in amazement at her earnest young face.

"He spent two whole years there," she'd continued breathlessly, happy to be telling me, to be telling someone, anyone at all. "He's shown us the pictures and everything. It's beautiful there. Did you know that Ndebele women, when they get married, paint the outsides of their houses with bright, geometric designs? That's what they're famous for, their painting and their beadwork. One day he brought in an Ndebele wedding apron made entirely of tiny colored beads. You should have seen it, Dad, each bead no larger than a piece of rice," she'd exclaimed, giving me a measure of it between two freshly painted nails.

Sitting there together last night, she'd told me all about the hippopotamus, Hippopotamus amphibious, citing fact after fact for me, as in a litany or prayer, only to end with a sharp, dramatic sigh. "It's the only class I like," she'd confessed to me, with the same fretful resignation I've heard so often in her mother. Indeed so alike is their expression these days, the moody way they speak, the moody way they fiddle with their bracelets and rings, that I often find myself at a loss to address her at all. For she has come to look a lot like her mother, too—her dark Sicilian eyes, her pouty, full-lipped mouth, her very way of sitting when she's lonely or anxious or sad.

It had been everything I could do to even guess what she was feeling last night, what she was feeling about me, about my father, reluctant as she'd been to talk about anything personal, about anything more than she could reach without strain. Only about school was she in any way forthcoming with me, complaining, in her offhand teenage way, that she was sick of it all, surely a common enough refrain, and one to which I'd done my best to respond with a kind if fatherly regard. She'd told me that the girls there were rich and snooty and that she hated the silly uniforms, the plaid skirts and high black socks that made her thighs and ankles itch. Above all, she hated the weekly chapel services and Masses, refusing, as a matter of principle, to sing along or pray.

When I'd asked her about her mother she'd told me her mother was fine.

I am scheduled to meet with the director of The Villas again this afternoon, to finalize the details of my father's move, and plan to bring Rachael along with me. No doubt she would prefer to spend the afternoon reading by the pool, though I'd like her to see the place, to see the room where my father will live. I feel I owe her this, this simple understanding of things.

When Rachael was younger we'd made a point of visiting my parents in Ithaca at least once or twice a year, driving up from Manhattan with a case of wine and a hamper of good city food: fresh bagels, smoked whitefish, Swedish wasabröd, and a few bricks of the smelly washed rind Limburger so favored by my father. They were mostly pleasant times, the five of us swimming in the lake, hiking the glen behind the house, and enjoying the occasional show at the Hangar Theatre in town. Then, much to my surprise, my parents had separated for a time, though I'd sensed no animosity between them, my mother returning to New York, to the Upper West Side, to finish her work on a series of articles she was writing on the author Vita Sackville-West and to renew her many friendships there, most of which had fared poorly during her years of living upstate.

She'd rented a furnished studio apartment just a block from the river by St. Hilda's, which she'd filled with her papers and books, and it was there and then that I'd gotten to know my mother as I'd never known her before. She'd been quite free with her words, dipping back into the past, whenever we'd met, with an ease, a candor, that had surprised me, tending as her stories had to be quite personal, though apologies, confessions, they were not. For she'd never expressed the slightest misgiving about the things she'd told me, never paused to measure my responses, never checked or amended her words. By her own explanation, she'd told me the things she felt I should know.

By then she'd given up trying to explain my father to me, to justify his behavior, had abandoned the notion that he and I might settle our differences at last, speaking of him and of the latest changes in their lives with a detachment, a forbearance, I could not, would not, share. To see my father objectively, by the terms of his own life, was not then possible for me, even if I'd been willing. We were much too proud, the two of us, much too close for that. Not that we'd ever really spoken, only eyed each other warily, each time I'd ventured home, whistling blithely to ourselves and colluding mutely with my mother who'd led us through the steps of our reunions like some soft-soled usher at church. He'd never asked about my work, never forgiven me, it seems, for the break I'd made from him, for rarely calling, for seldom coming home. For all he knew, I'd never read a one of his books, never wondered about his struggles, never stood for a moment in his cracked black shoes.

Still I'd been pleased to hear my mother talk about him, about our years together in Ithaca, to speak of the past without apology, opening it up to me again like the tale of some other family's life. I'd wanted her to know that it hadn't all been bad, that there were things I'd loved about the house, the town, that there were times with her, times even as a family, when we'd hiked the glens or gone swimming in the lake, that I remembered with fondness, relief. Most of all, I'd wanted her to know that I was happy, that I loved my work, my wife.

Yet even then I'd known that my marriage was failing. I was working longer hours than usual, travelling once or twice a month to Europe and Asia, and occasionally to South America, to Paraguay and Argentina, where my firm was beginning to press its concerns. Even when in New York I'd worked late most nights, getting back to the apartment long after Gina and Rachael were asleep. And though I'd told myself I couldn't help it, that my hands were tied, that our very happiness depended on it, I'd understood, each time I'd whispered goodnight to Rachael, each time

I'd curled myself around Gina in bed, that the terms I'd decried were my own.

It was my mother who'd told me that Gina was having an affair. I shouldn't have been surprised, surprised by the news, surprised that my mother had been the one to tell me of it, when it must have been apparent to everyone we knew. By then she and my father had retired here to Florida, the cancer still slumbering beneath her sun-warmed skin. How she'd known about Gina, I couldn't have said, only that I'd been forced to refute it to her face, where we'd sat together on the lanai, to feign indignation, to repudiate the facts, one by one, even as they'd swarmed like hornets in brain.

For it was hardly news to me that my relationship with Gina had cooled, that in the course of my many, often lengthy trips abroad we'd grown anxiously, dangerously, apart. By then we'd met rarely for meals, talked mostly by e-mail and cell phone, and scarcely ever had sex, but as a gesture of excess, so that I should have seen it coming. Hearing about it from my mother had only compounded the guilt, the anger, the pain, giving it a force, a poignancy I hadn't expected and laying me low for more than a week in Jakarta, where I'd returned to finish a job, before I'd found the strength to broach the matter with Gina herself.

There in Jakarta I'd fashioned my revenge: against my mother's advice, I'd determined to take Gina for all I could get—the apartment, the car, the house in Shelter Island, not to mention the custody of Rachael, whom I'd felt certain would shrink from her mother once she'd learned what she'd done. I'd stop at nothing, I'd resolved, eager to punish her soundly, to justify my anger, which had left me too weary, too sullen, to work, and had already spoken to my lawyer by the time I'd boarded the long flight home, thrilled by the thought of her disgrace.

Yet by the time I'd reached New York the fire had gone out of me. The flight from Frankfurt had been delayed so that it was late by the time I let myself into the apartment; nothing seemed changed. Gina had left the light on above the stove and briefly I'd rummaged around in the refrigerator, hoping to draw her from bed, to stroke her sleep-warm breasts, but she hadn't even stirred. Restless, sullen, I'd drunk a beer at the window, gazing down upon the empty schoolyard below, and wished I'd never come home.

RACHAEL HAD MADE REMARKABLY LITTLE fuss about our separation. Over the years she'd learned to conserve her emotions, meting them out with prudence, with care, so that when we broke the news to her one evening at our little French restaurant down the street she hadn't shed a tear, only folded her hands upon the freshly starched tablecloth and sighed.

For practical reasons, I'd agreed to be the one to move out, some many months later, when our attempts at compromise had failed, taking a small apartment across town in the same old brownstone in which one of Rachael's former teachers lived, or so we'd discovered one day when we'd stopped in the lobby to check the mail. I'd cared little about the particulars of the place—the number of bathrooms or closets, whether the floors were carpeted or tiled, eager only that Rachael should like it, that, whenever she was there with me, she should feel herself at home. And by and large she has. She loves the stamped tin ceiling in the kitchen, the built-in bookshelves, and the deep bay window in which she likes to sit and think.

I myself feel nothing for the place, its features—the pictures, the appliances, the carpets and TV—as drably compatible as those of any middling hotel suite. Whenever I'm there alone, the rooms press in upon me, even when I sleep, so that some nights I wake gasping in terror, only to puzzle dumbly at the noises in the street.

More than once, upon returning from a trip, I've given the taxi driver the wrong address, my old address, sometimes getting as far as the corner of 94th and Park before realizing my mistake.

Since I moved out, I've found it hard to settle down, to begin again, having lost all feeling for the city itself, for its shops and museums, for its restaurants and cafes, having lost all affection for our friends, who rarely call me now, averting their faces when I meet them in the street, so that I no longer experience the thrill of return at that first glimpse of Manhattan from the Triborough Bridge, but am all but stifled by dread. Whereas once I'd marveled at the city's gritty, indomitable spirit, at its sheer vitality, I can hardly wait to escape it now.

Only when Rachael is there in the apartment with me, when she is staying the night, does the city assume for me any semblance of home. She likes to play music and make popcorn, which we eat together before the TV. It is on the weekdays, when she is back with her mother, that I feel the weight of the city again and can hardly bear to enter the apartment, except to shower and change my clothes. On such nights I often work late in my office, ordering a sandwich from the deli downstairs or just picking at the remains of my lunch before curling up on the couch there to sleep.

Often while abroad I've imagined myself a different man. In one dream I return to New York on a late flight from somewhere—Ankara, Djibouti, Berlin—to find that my apartment has been robbed, emptied out like a shell. Nothing remains: not a book, not a can, not a teacup, a spoon. I picture the men as they carry out my bed, my bureau, hear them whistling through their teeth as they roll up the heavy Turkish rugs then heave them to their backs with a grunt. Thieves, they are not boors, but stop to look at the pictures on the walls: the photographs of Paris, the Japanese prints, between the windows in the kitchen Klee's cockeyed 'Head of Man', briefly appraising the checkerboard face—so tender, pathetic—before nodding their blockish heads. Of course the pictures are gone. The picture hooks, too.

Each time I return to find my things vanished I resist the urge to telephone the police, wandering the empty rooms like a prospective tenant, twisting the faucets, peering into the closets, and appraising the rooftops across the way. I order pizza with anchovies and garlic, which I eat on my bedroom floor, followed at once by an order of dumplings and fried rice from the restaurant down the street. It matters little where in the apartment I eat, even less where I sleep. The kitchen, stripped of intentions, is as good as the bedroom, the den. In every room I dream with ease, though never so deeply as to wonder why there is no one there beside me, no lover, no wife, never so keenly as to feel myself alone. Sated, safe, I fail to wonder at my life at all, at its future and past, at the clamoring call of the world out-side—the muted rumble of cars and buses, the boys from the projects playing ball in the street. Nothing draws me out; nothing keeps me in. Beneath the window the radiator hisses. Even the impulse to reason is gone.

It had been Rachael's idea, the first time she saw the new apartment, to paint her bedroom green, a soothing, chameleon-colored green that gave her the sensation, she'd once explained, of sleeping high in the branches of tall green trees on an island far away. And I'd known what she meant, as I've often found myself standing there in her bedroom doorway, when she's not there, absorbing the strangely hypnotic color of the walls and studying her girlish things, which inhabit their places in the cramped little room with the righteous fixity of jungle idols. For she is as neat as her mother is sloppy, her bed made, her desktop clear, her books arranged assiduously by subject and size. In her absence everything speaks of order, discretion. Yet just standing there lately I've sensed that something else is afoot. The air in her room is hot, moist; I hear the whispering of plants and recall the coyly self-conscious way she now looks at strangers, the way she purses her lips, the way she lifts her hair, exposing her long and lissome neck.

What is clear is that her beauty has already possessed her, this child of mine, has already laid its claim upon her hungry little heart. And her smell too has changed. No more the little girl, she hugs me some days, reeking of lip gloss and perfume. Whereas once she wore her heart on her sleeve with me, now she is cautious, on guard. And she's grown protective of her mother, even defensive, compelled by some burgeoning feminine instinct to restrict me to all but the most commonplace details of their life together, though I rarely ask about her mother anymore, not wishing to tread upon that private, hallowed ground.

Still, by the look on her face some days, I have to wonder what Gina has told her about me, about our marriage, about the annulment of our vows. I have to wonder how, by what coded female terms, she's described her infidelity to me.

Now some others have joined Rachael at the pool below—a dark, uniformed man with a skimmer and two elderly women in large straw hats with the leathery brown skin of some shell-less breed of tortoise. They are laughing, in this temperate autumn of their lives, slipping easily into the water in their bright floral bathing suits and paddling about with a placid satisfaction that stirs in me a vague if certain envy. No doubt their husbands are dead—or so their gestures seem to say. Their husbands are dead and they can swim without regrets.

THERE WAS A TIME, HE thinks, when I remembered such things: dates, appointments, names. That German woman who cleaned house for us—Adelhaid or Adelheid. So fat and pink, so nasty to the children. He chuckles. A mole the size of a quarter on her neck! There was a time when he remembered such things, when, perched high on a chair before his father's guests, he'd been able to recite the first fifty names and numbers from the Manhattan telephone directory only to reverse the trick. He remembers that. The promise, the thrill. And he remembers a time not bound by any other time when a man killed a pigeon in the street. Punted it like a ball, filling the air with feathers.

The last time I was here with Rachael I was here with her mother, Gina, as well. We'd been arguing for days and there'd seemed every reason to believe, when we boarded the plane in Queens, that our marriage would not survive the trip. Yet the warm gulf air had stirred something latent in us, so that by the time we'd arrived here we were talking again. Rachael, as if refreshed by the calm between us, had filled the night with laughter. And it hadn't ended there: I'd been awakened as in a dream the next morning by Gina's hand on my sex.

The day we'd arrived my father had just won a race as a novice sailor in the local regatta and was feeling good about the world, feeling good about himself, parading his little trophy through the apartment like some tawdry village saint, and joking easily with his red-faced fellow sailors whom we'd met for drinks and dinner at the club. Dressed handsomely in his navy blazer and clean white bucks, he'd been in high spirits that evening, crowing loudly about the race, and telling all with an ear to hear it about his service as a sailor in the Battle of Vella Lavella, so that one might never have guessed he'd once advocated the violent overthrow of these selfsame men and women who'd buzzed and chuckled about him at the bar, buying him drinks and teasing him about his dowdy little boat.

He'd treated us to lobster dinners that evening then drunk too much gin—or just enough to call out the demons in his head, until we'd been forced to escort him home, where he'd turned sullen with us, shutting himself in his room and refusing to emerge until morning.

By then, by the time he'd joined us at breakfast, humming merrily to himself, and duly anointed with his favorite bay rum, he'd seemed to have forgotten everything, the hectoring and recriminations, the lobster and gin, greeting us warmly, as he poured himself some coffee, and insisting that we spend the day sailing.

While at first Gina had demurred, not liking the idea of being trapped on a boat with my father, Rachael had been so keen on the idea that Gina had finally assented, when together we'd packed a lunch and trundled our way to the little marina, to the slip where my father kept his boat.

Back in Ithaca, he had purchased the second-hand sailboat, a 20' Nor'Star Pacific, a light, nimble craft in which he had spent many a happy day sailing the length of Lake Cayuga. He'd only agreed to move to Florida if he could bring the sailboat with him, which he'd managed to do, after much finagling, at a reduced if exorbitant rate.

The trusty little sloop had given him much pleasure in the years before my mother died. While usually he'd sailed alone, often returning to the marina just as it was getting dark, a habit that had caused my mother no end of worrying, they'd also taken frequent trips together, expressly romantic trips, to Captiva and to Cabbage Key, where on occasion they'd spent the night at the little inn there, in the Dollhouse Cottage, so that in time my mother had grown to enjoy her outings with him.

But for a few wisps of clouds that hung like spun sugar in the sky, the day was perfect for sailing when the five of us motored our way out of the marina then set sail through the slender sound that separates Pine and Sanibel Islands. My father was keen to show us Cayo Costa, one of the barrier islands just north of Captiva, to where he'd often sailed alone, and I remember the ease with which he handled the small craft, working the sheets and halyards like a master puppeteer. Hardly anyone spoke for the first hour, each lost in his own thoughts, when we were startled by a pod of dolphins off the bow.

We dropped anchor in a place called Pelican Bay, just beyond Useppa Island where in '61—so my father informed us—the CIA had trained a force of Cuban nationals for the Bay of Pigs invasion. As if to favor us, the breeze, quite stiff at times in our passage through the sound, had expired suddenly, smoothing out the bay like a hand on fresh sheets, so that for a while we paddled about in the clear green water before clambering back aboard to enjoy my mother's lunch.

My mother, made nostalgic by the wine, told Gina and Rachael the story of the time I nearly fell to my death while descending the steep temple steps at Teotihuacán. We'd been talking about the year my family spent in Mexico—about the people, the markets, the food.

My mother had been happiest in Coyoacán, in our small rented house overgrown with bougainvillea just a short walk from la casa azul. She'd loved the vibrant bohemian suburb of Mexico City with its bookstores and galleries, its plazas and cafes, and had often regretted the fact that they'd never returned.

My father, by contrast, had hated the place. He'd found it dirty and congested, the people pretentious, and had never grown accustomed to the bands of tourists—the Germans, French, and Japanese—that trooped from one site to another, day in and day out, from the house of Frida Khalo and Diego Rivera (in which brightly colored rooms they'd gawked at the former's paint brushes, orthopedic corsets, and China Poblana dress) to the crumbling refuge of Leon Trotsky where, for a substantial fee, they'd been permitted to see the desk at which the old Bolshevik was killed.

My father's book on Trotsky had been widely dismissed when it was finally published some five years after our return to the States, then swept aside by a tide of similar, more successful treatments of the Marxist's final days. It was a failure that had plunged my father into a deep depression, a well of morbidity out of which only gallons of gin and the precipitate purchase of the sailboat had been sufficient to raise him.

And raise him it had. Whereas he'd spent weeks in his bathrobe after the book's initial reception, staring glumly at the papers on his desk, he was suddenly out sailing by the time the sun was up each day, returning just before nightfall, eyes bright, cheeks flushed, his contempt for his critics renewed.

Yet my mother hadn't mentioned any of this while we were anchored there, in Pelican Bay, preferring instead to talk about our many sun-filled outings in Chapultepec Park and about the overgrown canals of Xochimilco with their garishly painted boats, called trajineras, on which we'd often amused ourselves in the company of the many well-dressed Mexican families that took their pleasure there on the weekends when the weather was fine. Merely describing the place had been enough to bring a smile to her eyes. For my mother had never taken to the life in upstate New York, with its tight-lipped locals and cold, gray winters that often stretched from September to May. She'd found the countryside oppressive with it derelict farms, scowling Indian reservations, and mud-spattered hamlets with neither parks nor gardens to draw the people out. Only when they'd retired to Florida had my mother seemed herself again, swimming daily, writing book reviews, playing bridge, and heading up the local Democratic Club before her cancer set in.

My father, never one to drink white wine, had helped himself to a second glass where he sat proudly in the stern that day, when, much to our surprise, as if completing a thought that had been blooming for years, he declared, "In the end he was just another despot." Of course he was referring to Trotsky. "That was the heart of my thesis, you see—his vanity and narcissism, his starring role in his own demise. Fiercely jealous of his place in history, he'd committed most of his energy, while in exile in Mexico, to redeeming his image abroad, which by then his rival Stalin had all but destroyed. He'd written articles, letters, pamphlets, and books; had arranged and given interviews; had broadcast a defense of himself by telephone to a capacity crowd in the old Hippodrome in New York; and had even gone so far as to stage his own show trial, in Frida Khalo's blue house, in the presence of reporters and friends—all in a desperate effort to clear himself of the many and exaggerated charges from Moscow. The consummate megalomaniac, he could think of nothing but his own vindication. And it was precisely there that he'd stumbled.

"Yes, for all of Trotsky's percipience," avouched my father

that day, as if to a class of wide-eyed freshmen, though in fact the sun and wine had made us drowsy and we were eager to go home, "for all his vaunted menschlichkeit, he'd overlooked the obvious, what was right before his nose: he'd neglected to attend to the people around him there in Mexico, to those very relationships that had saved and sustained him abroad. Is it any wonder he soon found himself gasping for air?" Clearly the question was rhetorical, my father taking the occasion to swallow the last of his wine, before grimacing briefly at the taste. "His time had run out, poor man. In his stubborn conceit, he'd alienated just about everyone he knew and his fate was effectively sealed. For by then the city was filled with Stalinist pistoleros and even his faithful Rivera and Kahlo had turned their backs on him."

He was about to continue when, turning abruptly to my mother, seated resplendently beside him, he whispered, "Do you remember the night we wandered over to his house on Avenida Viena and found it dark, the doors and windows bolted fast?" only to explain, looking first at me and then at Gina and Rachael: "Understand, we had only just arrived in Mexico, in Coyoacán, the nanny Maria was doing the dishes in the kitchen and the kids—you and your sister, David— were fast asleep. You remember, Natalya?" he pressed my mother once more, in a voice so pathetic, so rawly sentimental that even she seemed surprised. "Do you remember how warm it was that night, how we could smell the flowers blooming on the walls?" he pressed her gently, only to revert, with an upraised finger, to the pedagogue, the guide: "You see, Trotsky's grandson, Seva, was still living there at the time, though the house looked as though it had been shut up for years, overgrown with graffiti and barbed wire, and one might never have guessed that a whole world had ended there, inside, just over that crumbling wall…

"I of course knew it well, could picture the dusty little garden where the Old Man had tended his rabbits and chickens when he wasn't writing. He'd been mad about rabbits. Mad about gardening, too, the tranquil courtyard brimming with tropical plants and flowers—daisies, lilies, plantains, climbing roses, and cacti. It was uncanny, really, my feeling for the man, for his presence there that night. Here he'd been dead for some thirty years, yet somehow I'd expected to find a light on behind the wall, the old firebrand hard at work at his desk!"

At this, my father chuckled bitterly, perhaps embarrassed by his candor, and I was about to speak, to rescue him with the suggestion that we start back soon, when he scratched his chin and sighed. "That's the funny thing, how much the world has changed since then, how paltry our ambitions, how fleeting our claims to pride…"

Now with great effort my father levers himself out of his chair on the lanai, and, tempted as I am to help him, I know better than to move from my stool in the kitchen, and only watch him as he shuffles his way across the living room and down the hallway to the bathroom, when shortly I hear the fitful splashing of urine in the bowl.

TWO

I'D FIRST LEARNED of The Villas from a friend of mine, a fellow architect who'd recommended the place to me one day when he'd overheard me talking about my father. Not knowing what else to do, I'd scheduled an appointment to meet with the director, a plump, bespectacled young man who'd greeted me in the foyer with what had appeared to be a large red Bible in hand, an association I was never able to break in the course of my lengthy consultation with him that day, expecting him, each time he spoke, to bless me from Corinthians or some other such book, though the thick red volume had turned out to be nothing more than a mystery novel that one of the residents had misplaced.

Coincidentally, the director had spent a summer in Ithaca as a boy, living with his aunt by the lake, so that for a time we'd chatted easily about the town before returning to the matter at hand.

He'd recently seen to the completion of The Villas himself, he'd told me, thanks to the money left him by his mother, a large portrait in oils of whom I'd apparently overlooked in the busy Pelican Lounge. It was she who'd been responsible for the initial vision, he'd explained (a brilliant woman, a pity!), pressing me out into the muggy air to show me the verdant grounds. Eager, loquacious, he'd led me down around the empty swimming pool and gazebo to the newly expanded memorial rose garden with its frigid detachment of classical statuary, where briefly, perhaps for the sake of the names on the plaques at our feet, we'd sat swatting at the gnats before making our way back to the community center, by way of a wide cinder path, to admire his collection of Audubon prints ranged around the shallow-vaulted dining room like the Stations of the Cross.

He was proud of the place, it was clear, teasing the pretty young receptionist, adjusting the cushions on the chairs, and praising the local florist for her arrangement of lilies by the door. And he was proud of his various employees, introducing each member we met in a manner so crisp, so theatrical, I might have chuckled at the performance had but a one of them winked.

Not only was his staff well-trained in both traditional and alternative therapies, particularly those for residents, like my father, with LBD, but the facilities themselves reflected the very latest in geriatric science. He'd recently added a putting green, an aviary (in which a tiny, black-haired woman sat grinning amidst the parakeets), and a small auto shop with a brand new 413 piece tool set in which residents, whose inclinations were more mechanical, could tinker with the engine of a '69 Chevelle. He'd read it was good for the brain.

In the course of my visit that day I'd found there was much to recommend the place, each feature patiently, affectionately described for me, from the fully secured premises to the soft, muted colors and home-style furnishings to the innovative circular floor plan, so designed by the director himself, to prevent those who wandered from ever getting lost.

And he'd been full of pleasing terms and phrases—pride, dignity, and fulfillment, pleasing not so much because I'd believed or even fully understood them at the time, in the context, but simply because they'd suited my needs. They were the very words and phrases I'd flown from New York to hear.

We'd ended the tour in his office, a large, expressly impersonal set of rooms overlooking the rear parking lot. With its candy-striped upholstery, tiny electric coffee maker, and catalogue store paintings, it might have been a suite in some lonely salesmen's motel. Only the nameplate on the desk and the framed photograph of his son, a Marine sergeant recently deployed to Iraq, had proclaimed the office his own.

As I'd had no questions for him, that is, no questions he had failed to anticipate in the course of the tour, he'd introduced me to his computerized "affordability calculator" on which together we'd considered my father's current living expenses side by side with those of a comparable resident at The Villas. Not surprisingly, the fees at The Villas were competitive, if significantly so, considering "the spectrum of senior living options," "the sumptuous facilities and grounds," the "European-style dining," and the numerous "value-added services" included in the "modest monthly fees". Though I hadn't let on at the time, I wasn't concerned about the cost. What mattered only was that my father would be comfortable there, that I could trust that he was safe.

It was then that the director had sighed. "Hard thing,

this," he'd remarked to me at length, tapping the papers I'd just signed for him. For some reason I'd hadn't the will to leave just then and was grateful he'd had more to say. "Pets die, engines falter, trees come crashing down. It's the way of the world, it seems, but no one has to like it." Awkwardly he'd craned his neck and sighed, when, as if preparing to rise, he'd looked at me and smiled. "You know he won't get better."

"Yes," I'd said. "I know."

"They never do. It's the worst part of this job, really. They simply never do."

My mother had seen it coming, this day. She'd worried aloud to me one morning, not long before her cancer was detected, that my father would be incapable of caring for himself, of living on his own. "He just hasn't been the same," she'd confessed at length, adjusting her large white sunglasses where we'd sat together by the pool. She was still a beautiful woman, though I knew it would have surprised her to think so. "He loses things then weeps like a child. Just the other night we went to dinner at the club and he left his good sport coat behind. You know the one. Well, he simply collapsed in tears when he realized it, so confused, so dejected, that he could barely grasp it when I told him that the jacket had been found. I thought he would never be consoled, poor man, when, just like that," she'd said, snapping her fingers, "the mood was gone. It's like living with a stranger some days."

She'd been quick to blame herself for the change in him. She'd recently convinced him to sell his sailboat, a decision which, while ensuring his safety, had reduced him to shuf-fling about the apartment in his pajamas all day, griping about the construction across the street and complaining about his teeth. Sitting there in the sunshine that day, she'd insisted that my father was not the man he seemed to be. For all his boasting and bravado, he'd become increasingly needy of late, hanging on her every word and smile, shadow-ing her on her daily errands, and throwing tantrums if ever she contradicted him. She'd worried that if left to himself he'd forget to eat and sleep, that he'd simply give up on him-self, neglecting his medications and refusing to answer the telephone, the door.

In the weeks before she died she'd seen flocks of ravens in her dreams, heard the rings and knocking, seen my father floating dead and anxious above his chair. She'd admonished me not to try to care for him myself, as she'd suspected I might, insisting that, when the time was right, I place him in a suitable home. She'd made me promise her that, that I'd not be persuaded by him, that no matter what he argued I'd never acquiesce. Given half the chance, she'd warned me that morning, he would eat me alive.

INSOMNIA. HOMER. TAUT SAILS. HE thinks: My son intends to murder me, though he doesn't believe it, not really, thinks again of other things, of long waves and Mandelstam, of turbid, heaped up seas. He finds he cannot sleep, fears he hasn't slept for days, and gently untethers his mind (he pic-tures the hitch, the rusted cleat) until his thoughts rise up, no longer his own, sparkling just above him where he sits in his chair with the novelty of bubbles he might reach out and touch. But he doesn't dare, doesn't touch them, they appear so fragile, doesn't breathe for the warm, summery pleasure they give him, only watches them with his mind's bright, inexhaustible eye until all he has ever dreaded, all he has ever damned—that murky palimpsest scarred by tincture and gall—makes him snicker like a schoolboy at some impossibly filthy joke.

And snicker he does, so that his son looks up from his work in the kitchen to consider him (the faithful отец, the beloved paterfamilias!), cocks his head like he's heard a pheasant in the brush.

"How're ya doing, Dad?"

Head-deaf, he doesn't reply, refuses, something clenched tight in his chest, only samples the words that have scuttled to attention in his mouth, feels them as if they were actually there, the words, as if he could stick out his tongue in the mirror and see them, tiny little words all jumbled together at the tip: Just Me Sake For Leave God's Alone. For he has no intention of replying, to his son, to anyone anymore, immune, indifferent to such proprieties, such conventions, though he cannot stop the words from piling up in his mouth, has to swallow them, choke them down: footnotes, chapters, memos, psalms, great slopping soup bowls of skittish, satirical verse (nut-cracker, friend, idiot!) (o star of ox-eyed heaven!), has to suffer daily the lavish scalding of his throat, though he is no Aztec, the words no molten gold. The Aztecs? he puzzles briefly. Yes, the Aztecs and Cortés! For Cortés is precisely the point, he insists to himself, surprised, the very heart of what he is trying to see, to say, if only he could see and say it, if only the blasted fog in his head would lift long enough for him to distinguish the sylphid creaking of that conquistador's boots, to detect amidst the sweat and sulfur his tack and tooth-rot breath. But then he remembers: Cortés didn't wear boots. Not in the New World, never! He remembers the very lines from Díaz: "While Cortés was fighting, he lost a sandal in the mud and could not recover it. So he landed with one bare foot." One bare foot! So human, so real! The banality of it, the flies! Oh, the feculent stench of mud!

And that is all it takes, another shard in place, so that he giggles smugly, fingers tacky with glue, feels generous enough to adjudge without rancor this knave, his son, who has come to beseech him on bended knee, thinks with a trilling: *My head is awash with an iron tenderness*, feels ready to cleave his heart, to understand what that African, Pushkin, meant when he wrote: *I have outlasted all desire, /My dreams and I have grown apart...* when again he hears the sound. That sound! Through the blare of the television he hears it—Tink-swoosh, tink-swoosh—and is about to cry out when a face floats up before him.

"Dad, do you remember where this is?"

For a moment all he can do is gape at the face before him, at once familiar and strange: the thinning hair, the glinting silver glasses, the lightly stubbled lip. He knows the face well enough to be confused, is troubled enough by its waxy pallor not to speak too quickly, too soon. He senses a trick. "Have a look," he hears and suddenly there's a photograph to think of and the hand that holds it is his. For he sees the hand now, *his* hand: the spots, the bones, the reddish hairs clumped like sea grass on the leeward side of dunes. He sees the wrist, fleshless as a cam and groove, the arm a freckled pipe. Only then does he recognize the man in the photograph, the man who is him and not him, standing there in his bathrobe on a balcony (the dusty bougainvillea) in a place that could be anywhere but here, so that, once excited, he despairs of ever naming it, crushed and breathless where he sits, feels the failure like an abscess, a wound. The air grows hot and close; startled, he smells camphor, then lilies, and his eyes well up with tears.

In the album I've found the photo of my father standing on the narrow balcony of our house in Taxco, Mexico, a picture I took myself with my Hawkeye camera from the garden below. He doesn't appear to recognize it, mumbling irritably and shaking his head until I pry it from his grip, turning it to the light to better examine its detail, amazed afresh at its poignancy, at its ability to move me even now. For it has all come back to me: the damp, neglected garden, the reeking drainpipe, the rustic stone grotto with its scowling St. Jude. It is morning and my father has just emerged through the shuttered green doors of his study to smoke a cigarette and look down at the valley hazed over as in a dream by the scattered smoke of wood fires, a daily ritual as certain as the rising of the sun, which, at the moment the photograph was taken, was still obscured by the bat-infested cliff that overtopped our house.

In our year of living in Mexico my father had felt most at home in Taxco, huddled deep in the mountains of Guerrero, where in the market one day, in a fit of caprice, he'd purchased a grinning, man-sized calavera, made of some pale local wood, which he'd propped in the chair by his desk and called Posada. Through the wall that had separated my room from his makeshift study above the kitchen, I'd often heard him talking to the skeleton at night, before sleep overcame me, upbraiding it (*Death, be not proud, though some have calléd thee/mighty and dreadful…*), advising it (No, no, I'm afraid that won't do…), even consoling it when he himself was feeling low (You see, that's the thing about fear…).

He'd felt for the remote little town an affection he'd never felt for Cuernavaca or Coyoacán, let alone for New York, hiking the nearby hills in the afternoons, when the clouds amassed themselves in angry towers to the west, and sitting for hours over coffee and tequila on the brightly tiled terrace with our friend and neighbor, the Jewish doctor and communist, Arturo Cohen-Bravo, playing chess and arguing companionably over Gramsci, Menuhin's recordings with Furtwängler, and the war in Vietnam.

Fresh out of medical school, the doctor had had plans to improve the state of healthcare in Taxco when he'd first arrived there from Mexico City, few of which had ever been realized, he'd made a point of remarking to me one day where I'd found the anxious, birdlike man pacing back and forth before the geraniums on the terrace in one of his gaily colored guayaberas, as if the failure—so obscure to me—bloomed daily in his nerves. Yet one might never have known it. A wry, gregarious man (so lax in his discipline, so frivolous in his affections, that I'd often caught my father frowning at him), the doctor had liked to talk about French cheeses (for which he'd pined there in vain, the local shops carrying nothing but queso fresco and queso blanco), about the town's silver jewelry, and about the many celebrities he'd met in his year of practicing medicine there, the poets and movie stars and diplomats, occasionally recounting for us, at my mother's playful prompting, the story of his fateful encounter with the local hero, the world renowned silversmith, William Spratling, whose morbid acquaintance he'd made just twenty-three minutes after the American's fatal car crash on the outskirts of town.

At the time, my mother was studying Spanish and had occasionally taken me and my sister along with her to see her teacher, the three of us mounting the rickety stairs appended clumsily to the side of the old whitewashed hotel to the rooftop apartment where the kindly Sevillana lived with her blind French bulldog, her view of Santa Prisca, and her Egon Schiele nudes. Each time we'd climbed the wooden stairs she'd welcomed us with a sweet, spongy cake over which I'd squabbled bitterly with my sister, while my mother, in the voice of a child playing house, greeted strangers, shopped for fruit and socks, and ordered meatballs and a coffee for lunch.

Señora Cabreva had kept a phonograph in the back room there with an eclectic assortment of old records, 78s mostly: I remember a song called 'Sugar Shuckin' Blues' and Eddie Condon's 'Embraceable You', as well as a scratchy collection of gamelan recordings from Bali, a few of which she'd played for us on the rooftop one day, after she and my mother were through.

It was from there, high above the plaza that Christmas Eve, that we'd watched the last of the candle-lit posadas for which the town was famous. Señora Cabreva had invited us to celebrate the occasion with her, to sip hot chocolate and admire los peregrinos—the brightly costumed men, women, and children—as they wound their way through the narrow streets below, a tradition she'd insisted was hardly Catholic at all, but had its roots in the Aztec celebration of the birth of Huitzilopochtli. It was a thing she'd loved about the people there: their devotion—witting or not—to that ancient pagan god.

Initially my father had taken it upon himself to establish a useful routine for my sister and me, insisting that we make our beds and clean our rooms before breakfast each day, then pressing us to memorize certain poems by Wordsworth and Keats, after which he'd tutored us in a variety of household chores, teaching us to sweep and mop and do the laundry in the large cast iron sink out back. Yet, busy as he'd been with his own work, and impatient with our general recalcitrance, he'd soon grown weary of the task, settling at last for an hour of reading aloud to us before dinner each night from the classics he'd loved as a boy, from *The Odyssey* and *The Iliad* to the poems of Robert Louis Stevenson and *The Adventures of Sherlock Holmes*.

In the end there'd been blessedly little in Taxco to bind my sister and me to a schedule of any kind. Apart from our Tuesday and Thursday sessions with a sarcastic, hare-lipped tutor named Mr. Kane, during which we were drilled in mathematics and Greek and Latin roots, we were left largely to our own devices there, so that we'd spent whole days together dreaming beneath the laurels on the plaza, pilfering sweets from the stalls in the market, and wandering the roughly cobbled streets before the packs of mangy dogs like a pair of Mexican Pans.

Despite the difference in our ages, Lily and I had been closer that year than at any time before—or since. People had often mistaken us for twins for the way we'd mirrored each other's moods, adjusting automatically to one another, and with the finest calibrations, so that, while together there in Taxco, things had rarely seemed amiss. It was only when we'd fallen into the company of others, as we sometimes had in our peregrinations through the rugged, hillside town, only when our parents had called us home for dinner or when Mr. Kane had set us at odds with each other over a list of Latin roots that the chord that bound us had come undone.

Even then Lily had sensed too much of the world, her daily experience of it so acute, so visceral, she'd literally trembled with the feelings of others. Always an anxious child, she'd hated it when my parents fought and had nearly burst from her skin one day when the neighbors slaughtered a pig in their yard. Once, in Cuernavaca, when briefly I'd been hospitalized for a concussion after tumbling from our garden wall, she'd come to visit me in my room in the converted old hacienda, and had been so overwhelmed by the pain in the air, by the decades of suffering still alive in the tiles, the walls, that my mother had had to take her home.

Since then, since our return to the States, I have often tried to remember that year through Lily's eyes, to substantiate it for reasons of my own. If I try I can picture her bedroom there in Taxco, a cold and gloomy little chamber just down the hallway at the top of the stairs; I can see the heavy velvet drapes that covered the window, smell the sweet, waxy scent of the wardrobe by her bed. What I can't recover, what

I can't conceive of at all, is the fact she was miserable there. For so she has insisted, time and time again, explaining to me—almost pleading the words—that she was wretched there, that year, often crying herself to sleep.

She'd told me many such things, once we'd returned to the States, including the story of an old man with a parrot who'd had the most beautiful voice when he'd sung her 'Las Mañanitas' in the square. He'd painted his old guitar (Didn't I remember it?) with a simple mountain scene of donkeys with large covered loads on their backs. Surely I remembered his shiny silver teeth, she'd pressed me fervently, though I'd remembered no such man or parrot, and have often wondered how and when she'd met him, if indeed she'd ever met him at all.

She'd had a friend there, too, she'd claimed, a pretty little girl in pigtails whose sister was a ballerina and collected the most beautiful dolls, though I cannot recall any such girl or friendship, any such sister or dolls. Then there was the time, Lily had told me, when our father had spanked her before a house full of guests, nicking his hand on the edge of the table and bruising her thigh. While I have no recollection of that either, I can surely recall his temper, the way it had simmered for days before exploding at the slightest provocation, forcing Lily and me to seek shelter in our rooms until our mother called us out.

It's Taxco, he chirrups. Mexico! **Cortés!**

It was there in Taxco that my father had completed the final draft of his book on Trotsky, working from five to nine each morning before making his way down the steep, cobbled streets with their broken flights of stairs to his favorite café just off the Plaza de la Borda for a coffee and roll, followed always by a short glass of beer. It was the only café, positioned as it was at the end of dank and narrow alley filled with feral-looking cats, where he'd been assured of never finding Americans, though the place was clean and the view of the valley fine.

For the town that year had teemed with Americans, with artists and students and retirees who'd seemed to do little more each day than wander listlessly through the streets, ambling past the innumerable platerías, with their cheerful young touts, and stopping here and there to squint in the sunlight before the large glass jars on display in the many small restaurants off the plaza, from one of which, on occasion, they would treat themselves to a glass of agua fresca before tracking their illusions down another cobbled lane.

My father had hated the sight of them, his compatriots, refusing to attend their weekly game nights and soirées, which he'd claimed were designed for nothing more than the swapping of wives and the witty denigration of the very Mexicans who cooked their food, cleaned their houses, and scrubbed their garish clothes. If he was ambivalent about Americans while back in the States, he hated them abroad, rebuffing their greetings in the street and insisting to my mother, who was duly loved by them, that she never bring them home.

It was a position that had baffled me then, and in the years that followed, when we'd returned to the States. I couldn't fathom his bitterness, his hatred of virtually everything American, confused and embarrassed by the way he'd taken issue with the simplest, most commonplace things: the fast food and shopping malls, the advertisements on television, the flagpole and flag in our neighbor's front yard. At my baseball games he'd refused to sing the national anthem, standing defiantly with his hands at his sides, and had taken my teacher to task one day for requiring us to say the Pledge of Allegiance at the start of her class.

Proud, pedantic, he was unlike the other fathers I knew, men who drank beer, enjoyed football, and gathered weekly at the Masonic Lodge. He didn't like camping or picnics, never wore blue jeans or shorts, and rarely left the house without a jacket and tie. He didn't hunt or bowl and never tinkered with cars, generally abjuring the company of others—men and women alike—to sit alone in the yard, stroking the binding of some book, his eyes lost upon the long, gray lake.

The truth was that he'd never really had any friends, none I knew of anyhow, only colleagues, associates—anxious, sallow-eyed men with their beards and pipes, who'd treated him, on the rare occasions when I'd had the chance to meet them, with a clear, if cautious respect. Not that my father had ever seemed lonely; when he wasn't busy in his office on campus, he was often hard at work in his study downstairs.

I'd known very little about him then, for he'd rarely talked about his past, about his childhood in New York, about his life as a man in the years before I was born, the only hard clues an old yearbook from the Ethical Culture School, in which a number of his teachers and classmates had signed their names; a star-shaped Navy Medal of

Honor; and an old Titenschreiber pen. They were the only relics of his former life to have survived his own purges, for he was always cleaning, always throwing things away, ever eager to reinstate order in our undisciplined lives, ever outraged by the insidious accumulation of material things.

But for his books and papers, there was nothing he'd collected, nothing he'd coveted, nothing he'd saved. Even his library had been subject to a yearly pruning. For it was not uncommon for him to spend hours in his study at the back of the house, visibly weighing the volumes in his hands in his attempt to determine which he would keep (which were essential to his work) and which (indulgences finally) he would dispose of, donating them, as was his custom, to the library in town.

It was this, his hostility to material possessions, to the randomly assembled iconography of a personal past, that had quickened in my sister and me an affection for physical tokens of the lives we were living, a passion for keepsakes and mementos, a hungry, nearly spiritual reverence for things. And like a miser I'd hoarded my possessions—my pencils and sketchbooks, my jackknives, guitar picks, and tapes, guarding them against my father's incursions, which were as ruthless as they were random, so that gradually the simple objects had assumed to me the power of talismans, masking themselves to my father's eyes, when of a Saturday morning he prowled my room in search of "superfluity", and protecting me from what, at the time, had seemed like calculated attempts to annihilate me.

Once, when I'd exploded in frustration after one of my father's raids, my mother had sat me down in my room and rubbed my back until my anger at him had passed and I was cross at myself instead, ashamed at my perennial weakness with him, at having allowed him to hurt me once again. That day she'd told me a little about his childhood, more than I'd ever heard before, about his taciturn mother, about his stern, censorious father, insisting to me, in a way that had seemed like pleading, that he was a good man, my father (Why else would she have married him?), and that he loved me very much. She'd said she hoped one day I might forgive him his judgments, that I might find myself grateful for the choices he'd made.

And I had. Even before I'd left for college I'd recognized my debt to him, had internalized his all but sacred bequest, carrying myself, by the start of my senior year, with an arrogance, a presumption, that had astonished my teachers and peers. While often my father had extolled the locals there, insisting that they were the good, true people, the very salt of the earth, he'd taught me to despise them, too, to pity them their ignorance and servility, their filthy nails and teeth. No fools, the locals had pitied my father in kind, often mocking him behind his back. Each year they'd amused themselves by inviting him to join their clubs and teams, to go ice fishing with them, to shoot pool in one of the working class bars in town, even importuning him one summer to march with his fellow veterans, in full regalia, in the Fourth of July parade.

Yet it hadn't stopped there. Once, after my father had mentioned that he liked the taste of venison, they'd strung a dead buck from a tree in our yard that had twisted there for a week before my father cut it down.

Even my father's colleagues—wry, learned men from Chicago, Stuttgart, and Oxford—had soon grown weary of him and his overbearing ways, rarely consulting with him at work and declining my mother's invitations to our home. It was a consensus, in the tightly-knit town, that had cast a shadow over my sister and me, so that initially we'd taken to disparaging our parents out loud, making sport of them to our classmates and neighbors until we'd trembled with the shame of it and the only alternative had been to despise the locals themselves.

And despise them I had, even as I'd cursed my father for his snide, superior ways. Appalled by my peers, by their drugs and their music, and by their greasy-eyed girlfriends who'd idled vainly by their cars after school, I'd kept to myself that year, excelling in my classes, reading everything I could find, and often staying late to finish my work. For I'd learned my lessons well. I was bound for better, greater things, and looked with pity on the people there, my class-mates and neighbors and friends, blinded, hobbled as they were by their listless satisfactions, by their void and bum-bling faiths. The fatalism and poverty, the cringing, obei-sance, and truckling—I would break free of it all.

For that I'd had my father to thank. Yet even then, and for all my contempt for the people there, I'd known that some-thing was wrong, something missing—in my father, in my family, in me. It wasn't church or God; what I'd envied in my friends and classmates was something else, something not so much spiritual as cultural, structural. At their best, and for all their futility, my friends had seemed lucky, fortunate, to me with their Hail Marys and bar mitzvahs, with their tatty Irish pride, emerging into the world some days with a clannish self-possession that had left me dejected, bereft.

When once I'd asked my father where we came from, what people, what place, his reply to me had been plain: "The only thing that matters is who you are now."

He'd said it, I remember, without a hint of irony, though he himself was haunted by the past—by his relationship with his father, by the Holocaust, by the very history he read and wrote, wrung so dry some days he'd barely had the strength to eat. Rootless, bitter, he'd seemed possessed to me, pacing the creaky floor of his study at night and cursing his many ghosts.

I'd always known my father as an angry man, though I'd never been able identify the source of his rage, to trace it back, to unravel its many and tangled threads. Since my earliest conception of him, he'd existed for me in a protracted present tense, spurning tradition and God, as he had, and abridging the universe to suit his simple conjugations of the glorious Here and Now. He'd seemed to me a man outside of time itself, a spectator merely, some rare, unearthly, at times magnificent creature who'd stalked defiantly through my days, pausing now and then to consider the drama of living with the animadversion of a god. And like the God of the Jews my father had been all but featureless to me, though as a child I'd seen him each day. Had I been pressed to describe him to a stranger, to draw a portrait of him in art class, to make him the subject of a weekly report, I'd have balked at the task. Even when I'd been tempted to speak of him to my mother, to lament his indifference to me, to make an open ally of her, I'd never been able to find the terms to describe him, to pin him down, to fully hate him or embrace him, the requisite words and phrases as elusive, as ineffable, finally, as the very names of God.

Life for my father was a grave matter, so that he'd had little time for simple things: for school plays, for scraped knees, for vacations by the sea. Like a prophet of old, he'd looked upon the world with a mixture of reprehension and scorn, damning the profligate, the lazy, the weak of will, and oppugning folly at every turn—and all with a righteousness that had made me grateful to him, whenever he'd taken an interest in me, for indulging the caprices of my kind.

Of the Americans there in Taxco he'd been particularly critical, going so far as to upbraid them as a lot one day in an editorial he'd submitted to the local paper. There'd been something protective, even nostalgic, about his feelings for the wayward little town, and briefly there'd been talk of buying a house there and settling down for good. For with each passing month in Taxco my father had grown more anxious, more irritable, at the thought of returning to New York. It had taken him only a few drinks in the company of friends before he'd turned vociferous in his criticism of the U.S., lambasting Nixon, Kissinger, and Agnew for their reckless policy in Vietnam and for their cynical war against the Left at home, a secret strategy designed to isolate and undermine the student leaders, clergy, trade unionists, and liberal Democrats who'd recently joined forces in an effort to bring the war to a swift and precipitous close. On one occasion he'd gotten so angry after reading an editorial in the *Herald Tribune* that he'd torn his passport to bits.

Some friends of my mother's had made it known to her one morning, when they met her in the market in town, that they were planning to sell their house just up the hill from us and move back to Kansas, the news of which had instantly invigorated my father. At once he'd tallied up their meager savings and put in a call to his bank in New York to see about taking out a loan against the vacant beachfront property in New Jersey that he and his sister had inherited from an aunt in Cape May, and all without consulting my mother who'd exploded one morning, smashing her coffee mug on the terrace at his feet.

"Have you completely lost your mind?" she'd demanded, in a tone that had brought me running to the window, for, though they'd often argued, she'd rarely lost her temper with him. That it was first thing in the morning had made the confrontation especially strange. "You're a coward, Jacob Ansky. That's what it is. You're afraid to go home. You're afraid to face facts."

"Good morning to you too, my dear," had come my father's unctuous reply. As usual at that hour, he'd been reading the newspaper over coffee on the terrace, and briefly, as if indulging the tantrum of a child, had lowered his paper to look at my mother, peering sardonically over the top of his half-moon glasses. "Facts? And what facts might they be?"

From my place at the window, I'd looked directly down upon his tonsured head, its appearance from there so egg-like, so fragile-looking, I'd wondered it had never been cracked.

"You read the papers every day, you tell me!" my mother had countered deftly, rooted firmly where she'd stood at the top of the terrace steps. "What is it that frightens you so?"

For a moment my father had studied her in silence, when, convinced that she was serious, that she wasn't going to leave him in peace until he answered her, he'd folded up the newspaper and set it beside him on the table, tapping it gently with his fingertips so that for a few moments the air had buzzed with the tension between them. So great was the suspense that I'd nearly called down to greet them, anything to break the silence, when dramatically my father had sighed.

"The country we knew as children is gone," he'd begun slowly, deliberately, if without a hint of his usual condescension. He'd seemed genuinely aggrieved. "And I don't mean changed; I mean gone, as in vanished, bought and sold, consumed. While surely the trappings remain—the symbols, the rhetoric, the myths—the country you speak of, Natalya, the country to which you wish so keenly to return, is but an illusion now, a painted set propped up by rich men and their lackeys to distract us while they wage their filthy wars and rob our children blind. I refuse to pretend it is otherwise." And there he'd raised a finger to prevent her from interjecting. "And, yes, lest you think I exaggerate, let me ask you this: Can you picture your David a soldier? Can you see your son at war?

"For there will be another war, Natalya; of that you may be sure," he continued softly, turning his coffee cup in his hands. "When this one ends, and it will end one day, there'll be another, maybe two, to replace it. Yes, soon there'll be a brave new war, a bold new junta of politicians, fat cats, and generals eager for fresh recruits," he'd pressed my mother that day, when he'd looked at her and frowned. "What will you say when they come for your boy? Think hard about it, Natalya, for even now the engines are whirring: Gaza, Cambodia, the Suez Canal. Even now the generals are clicking their teeth."

My mother, taken aback by the question, had shifted her stance on the terrace below me, arms folded tightly across her chest. I couldn't guess what she was thinking, her eyes wide and mouth set, as if too angry, too puzzled to speak.

Sensing his advantage, my father had made one more sally to drive his point home. "Surely you wish your David to be happy," he'd declared to her, "to be safe from harm, to be free to live as he chooses. Of course you do, but there's the rub, you see…"

"No! No!" my mother had wailed suddenly, pulling at her hair. "No, I don't see. I don't agree with you at all. This has nothing to do with David. Nothing at all. It's about you, Jacob. You! It's about the fact that you're scared, scared to test your theories, your mettle, in the only place it matters anymore, back there, in the thick of things," she'd assailed him, jabbing angrily at the valley below. "That's what this is all about, isn't it? This house, this town, this precious little reverie of yours? You'd rather sit here in safety, here on your quaintly tiled terrace with your coffee and rolls, where nothing you do can fail, where nothing you say can be checked. Well, I'm sick of your diatribes, Jacob, sick of your ranting and raving. I mean, look at you—still in your bathrobe at eleven o'clock in the morning!" And there she'd hesitated. "If only your father could see you now…"

At her words my father had leapt to his feet, as though electrified. "My father? Don't you ever compare me to my father!" he'd thundered back at her, jabbing a finger in her face. I'd never seen him so angry; even from above him I could make out the color in his neck. "My father didn't give a damn about his children, didn't give a damn about his wife. Don't you ever compare me to that man!"

Remarkably, my mother hadn't flinched at his reaction, holding her ground, though he'd towered above her in rage. For she'd had more to say, looking him hard in the eyes and shaking her head. "I should have seen it coming. This book of yours, this trip. For years you've been trying to escape."

"What are you talking about, escape?" Indignant, he'd all but hissed the word at her, though just by the way he'd stood there adjusting his robe I'd sensed that my mother had won.

"Ever since I met you, Jacob, you've been trying to get away, squandering your prospects, spurning your friends and colleagues, and burning every bridge you cross. The moment things start going well for you, for us, you find a way to sabotage them. And all because you're scared, scared to face up to things, hunkering down here in Mexico as if it's an act of conscience, of courage. Talk about illusions! Just look around you. This," she'd exclaimed, gesturing vaguely at the house, the hills, at the pigeons on the rooftop next door, "all of this is nothing but a dream in your head, a delusion! And here's the real rub, Jacob: you're willing to sacrifice your own children to feed it.

"Well, I'm not," she'd concluded abruptly, stooping to collect the fragments of her mug, only to stop at the head of the stairs to consider him once more. "If there's work to be done back home, I want my children to do it—on their own terms, in their own imperfect ways. For better or worse, it's the only home they've got."

My father has found a ballgame on the television; I can hear the sportscasters and the rhythmic chanting of the crowd, and decide that while he's distracted I'll have another crack at his room, at sorting the last of his things.

At Gina's suggestion I'd hired an estate agent some months ago to dispose of the furniture, once my father is out: the beds and dressers, the bookshelves, couches, and tables, as well as the gaudy old service of Meissen china that my mother had been unable or unwilling to sell before their move to Punta Rassa. Only the clearing out of my father's den have I reserved for myself, though, since my arrival yesterday, I've avoided the dank little room where his presence hangs so heavily I find it difficult to breathe. I've never liked touching his things, which even now, now that he is helpless, seem charged with anger, reproach.

As a child it was only rarely that I'd ever ventured into his study alone. The room had been strictly off limits to my sister and me, so that I'd had to screw up my courage each time before pressing my way in. I remember that everything about the room had seemed weary to me—the books and chairs, the lamps and carpets, the ugly green wallpaper he'd never bothered to have replaced. He'd rarely opened the windows, with their watery gray panes, so that the air itself had seemed spent, as though it had been breathed and exhaled a thousand times before. I'd hated the musty, dry smell of the place, that stale compounding of tobacco and dust that had seemed to permeate my very flesh, so that for days afterwards I'd smelled it on my skin, no matter how I'd scrubbed, a scent so distinctive, so damning, I'd feared my father himself might detect it.

Yet for all of this, I'd been unable to resist the urge to study his things: his books and papers, his pens and pencils, sitting gingerly before his typewriter and tapping at the keys. He was a failure, I knew. His trappings had told me so: the marble paperweight, his squeaky chair, the basket of old carbon paper, the sheets wrinkled and faded like skin. I'd known it for years, had sensed it at least in the way he'd skulked about the house on the weekends, and in the way that my mother had spoken of him to our neighbors and friends, bragging about his daily triumphs—a nail here, a little glue for the arm of a chair—as if there was nothing left for a man like my father to do.

His room off the kitchen here is dark and I open the blinds at once, squinting at the harsh white light. The smell in the air is pungent, human, unmistakably his. The bed is too large for the space, the small white desk, with its cumbersome computer, cocked at an angle beneath the window so that there is hardly room to move. Gathering up the dirty tissues on the floor, I replace his books, mostly cheap paperbacks that he's left strewn about the room, then empty the cracked Hôtel Vendôme ashtray, packed to overflowing with cigarette butts, when, in a gesture that fills me with grief, I strip the sheets from his bed.

For all I know, it has been weeks since he's slept in the room, yet I feel compelled to make up the bed for him, for his last night at home, rooting around in the hallway closet until I find what I need.

What remains in the room is mostly sentimental—the prints and photographs, the time and tide clock, the antique map of St. Petersburg on the wall by the door. The tall wicker bookcase is all but bare.

It had been my father's idea, when he and my mother moved here from Ithaca, to dispose of his library, and I remember how indifferent he'd seemed to the prospect of selling off the hundreds of volumes he'd collected over the years, including many rare, once-treasured histories in Cyrillic dating back to the reign of Peter the Great. I'd driven up from the city for the weekend to help them pack and had been amazed at the ease with which he'd disposed of his once-precious books, barely glancing at each before tossing it—like a potato or ear of corn—onto one of the piles on the floor.

My mother had urged him to donate the books to the university library, where they might be enjoyed by students and faculty for years to come, but he would have none of it, arranging for the sale of them—some eighty-nine boxes worth—to a bookseller in Rochester who'd appeared at the house, one crisp winter morning, loaded them into his truck, and promptly vanished before a cloud of blue smoke.

Now all that remains of my father's collection, besides some boxes in storage downstairs, are a few titles in Russian, Hilberg's *Destruction of the European Jews*, two books on chess (*100 Soviet Chess Miniatures, The Immortal Games of Capablanca*), his trusty *Chapman Piloting, Seamanship & Small Boat Handling,* and a heavily annotated edition of his father's controversial defense of Stalin first published in Paris in 1953, which I am unable to read in the French, restricted instead to perusing my father's cacographic glosses that clutter the margins like weeds.

The last time I was here I'd helped him to organize his files, such as they were, and to balance his checkbook, simple tasks over which he'd fretted helplessly, though I'd long ago assumed responsibility for paying his bills. He'd kept a shoebox beneath his desk for his various receipts, his counterfoils and chits, which we'd emptied onto the kitchen table one morning, matching each slip—each bar tab and incidental—against his monthly statements from the bank. And he'd felt better for it, thanking me suddenly, when we rose from the table, with a brief if solicitous hug.

It had been my mother's idea, when my father was first diagnosed with dementia, only months after his heart attack and surgery, to create a dummy account for him at the bank, for it had become clear to her that he was no longer capable of managing their finances. After years of dependence on him, she'd had to learn to pay the bills herself, to balance the checkbook, and to fill out their yearly income tax form—pat, perfunctory skills she'd acquired so quickly it had amazed her to think they'd caused him such grief. Yet she'd never judged the man, sitting patiently beside him at his little desk each month as he'd scribbled out the checks, then addressed the envelopes, one by one, in his slack and trembling hand.

I find the large drawer of his desk stuffed with lottery tickets, old credit card statements, and a few tightly bound packets of cancelled checks from their former bank in Ithaca. There too, still in its velvet case, is the Patek wristwatch I gave him for his birthday, some years ago, as well as a boxed draft of his last book, what was to be his magnum opus, a sweeping cultural history of modern Russia, which he'd never managed to complete, having agonized so long over the life and fate of the poet Osip Mandelstam that finally he'd abandoned the project in despair.

What little else remains in the drawer is junk and I dump it into a garbage bag without sorting it, quickly sealing it with a twist to prevent my father from fussing.

During my last visit, some months ago, I'd been awakened in the middle of the night to find him rifling desperately through the bags I'd filled with my mother's things. Kneeling there in the living room amidst her handbags and shoes, he'd berated me for my callousness, for my "cunning indifference to death," a trait—so he'd claimed to me that night—he'd seen budding in me for years. He'd insisted on keeping the shoes and purses and flower print smocks, refusing to return to bed until I'd replaced them in her room. It had come as a surprise to me, therefore, when I'd peeked into my mother's closet yesterday, to find it empty, even her baskets and hangers gone.

His own closet is really all that remains to be cleared out before tomorrow. Behind the sliding doors, beneath his shirts and blazers and musty woolen suits, I find his old Dopp kit, complete with safety razor and brush; his favorite Nunn Bush oxfords, cracked and misshapen by wear; two crates of paperback mysteries; a couple of empty shoe trees; and, still secure in its case, his trusty Hermes 3000 typewriter, the angry chatter of which I can hear even now. So sharp is the memory of it that I cannot resist the temptation to have a look at the old portable, setting it on the desk before me and fingering its pistachio-green keys.

It is much as I remembered it, if smaller, lighter, so that it is easy to quicken the image of my father hunched before it late at night, as I'd often found him when I'd stumbled from bed for a drink. He'd written more in our years in Ithaca than in any other time in his life, a seemingly inexhaustible stream of books and articles and Letters to the Editor that had poured from his typewriter as from an underground spring, the simple machine then so miraculous to me that for a time I'd actually imagined a hole in the desk there beneath it.

Then, he'd seemed heroic to me, my father—strong, courageous, battling evil and inequity wherever he'd found them, his aloofness and occasional cruelty to me the very marks of his valor.

I remember he'd hated a man named Pipes, a prominent historian and Cold Warrior at Harvard, who'd once accused him, in an editorial in *The New York Times*, of being an apologist for Soviet terror, the very charge that had been levied so successfully against his father, just decades before, destroying his career and forcing him into exile in France. From that point on my father had gone to war with Pipes, writing editorial after editorial, essay after essay, in his effort to counter the man's contentions, as well as to undermine his scholarship, which—so my father had claimed—was not only methodologically flawed but blindly polemical as well, at best a caricature of Soviet life. Detesting Stalin as my father had, it could not have been an easy position to argue, but there I'd found him each night, between Skylla and Kharybdis, charting his lonely way.

To the best of my knowledge, he'd never made peace with

his father following his return from Paris, had never forgiven him for his "pigheaded politics," for abandoning the family when they'd needed him most. By then he'd come to detest his father's idealism, a faith so blind, so hidebound, that not even Stalin's most flagrant betrayals—the Great Purge, the Ribbentrop-Molotov Pact, The Night of the Murdered Poets—had been sufficient to shake it. It was only after his father was dead and gone that for a time he'd tried to make his amends with him, defending him in public, while poring over his papers in private in an effort to understand the fervid, once-illustrious man.

On only two occasions can I remember my father ever mentioning his father to me, the first, some years ago, when he was staying with us in our apartment in Manhattan, when apropos of nothing he'd told me about the time the man had cursed him like a dog before his friends. He'd been drinking, my father, his voice thick with feeling where I'd found him standing at the large plate glass window in the living room, gazing out over the city, over the hapless, gray projects of Harlem and the Bronx. He'd offered me a drink but the bottle was empty.

The only other time he'd ever spoken to me of his father was just last night, when I'd surprised him in the midst of an argument so fervent, so impassioned I'd thought there was someone in the bedroom with him. Of course I'd realized my mistake too late. The instant I'd opened the door, he'd turned to me, eyes struck wide with terror, only to groan in despair. For he'd been arguing with his father, so much was clear, rebutting him at last with that clipped and mor-dant trenchancy that can only come from years of patient rehearsal. I should have recognized the tone, the stakes. Face contorted, he'd merely stammered at me in pain: "He was afraid for me, the…the bastard! Afraid for me!"

What little I know of my grandfather, Joseph, was told me by my mother, who'd always felt an abiding affection for the blithe, tempestuous man. It was she alone, when she and my father were first married, who had traveled to Paris twice a year for three years running to see my grandfather, where he'd taken a gloomy apartment in Saint-Germain-des-Prés, she alone who had crossed the Atlantic to bring him the latest news of his family when his grieving wife was forbidden to travel and his son—my father—refused to utter his name.

My mother had enjoyed telling me about the unusual friendship that had developed between the two of them in that fabled city, about his kindness to her, about their walks along the Seine. Summer there was hot, muggy. Hungry for perspective, for air, they'd taken the lift to the top of the Eiffel Tower one day, from where they'd gazed out over the smoldering city, each rapt in his thoughts. For there were occasions, she'd told me, when he hadn't spoken for hours, as if, after a lifetime of wielding words, he'd suddenly had no use for them at all.

At the time my grandfather was still writing for the *Daily Worker*, making regular trips to Cuba, China, and Indo-China to meet with fellow Communists, and diligently editing the occasional proof or manuscript that was sent his way, but his heart was no longer in it. Still he'd done his best to please my mother, each time she'd made the trip to see him, showing her the sights of Paris and sitting with her in his favorite restaurants each night where he'd watched her without eating, content with his cigarettes and gin.

Always he'd been kind, even fussy in his attentions to her, opening doors and pulling out chairs, though the change in him was plain. By then, by the time of my mother's visits, my grandfather was a broken man, his back stooped, his eyes—once flashing—a flat and dirty gray. He'd missed his wife and children terribly and had deeply regretted the time he'd lost with them, often fretting aloud to my mother the list of things he'd left undone. And he'd confessed to her, one bright winter day as they'd strolled through the Tuileries, that he'd taken a mistress. For this he'd made no excuses, no apologies to the slender young woman at his side, only frowned at the fact of it, twisting his calfskin gloves.

By the time I'd gotten to know my grandfather he'd been nothing but a shell of his former self, his pomp and bluster but shadows on a screen. His wife was dead, the *Daily Worker* defunct, the American Communist Party crushed and discredited. What's more, no newspaper would hire him, so that he'd been forced to earn his living until he died by doing odd jobs, mostly painting and carpentry, and by editing technical articles for a professional journal out of Philadelphia called *The Dental Times*.

The man who'd returned from exile in Paris had been a far cry from the man my mother had met when my father first brought her home with him to their spacious Upper West Side apartment. Professional Communist, imperious foreign editor for the *Daily Worker*, Joseph Ansky had charmed her at once with his heady, quixotic blend of politics and passion. He'd talked late into the night, the first time they'd met, about his dream—still ripe in him then—of building a truly revolutionary world community, pulling books off the shelves in eager attestation of his plan and refilling her glass with fine French wine until she felt she was floating free and weightless on the mighty current of his words.

Even as a student at City College my grandfather had exuded such confidence, such vision, that he'd infuriated his professors and made all the girls swoon. With his broad shoulders, thick black hair, and fine square jaw, he'd not only been exceedingly handsome but a bold and charismatic speaker as well. It was my mother who'd told me of the occasion, described to her by her mother-in-law shortly after she and my father were married, when, as a younger man, my grandfather had been giving a speech at an anti-Fascist rally in front of the New York Public Library when he was charged by the police, who'd literally torn off his clothes in their effort to subdue him. "He was a fighter, your grandfather. Refusing to surrender, to cut short his address, he slipped like an eel from the policemen's grasp and shimmied half-naked up a nearby flagpole from where, to the delight of his fellow activists, and much to the amazement of the crowd, he finished his speech before sliding back down!"

Having grown up the daughter of a real estate broker in Larchmont, New York, my mother had never met a family like the Anskys with their radical politics, biting sarcasm, and fine antique rugs. If there was someone to know, Joe Ansky had known him, as the photographs in his study had attested, his friends and acquaintances ranging from Khrushchev and Ho Chi Minh, to Kennedy and De Gaulle, to Arthur Koestler, Edward R. Murrow, Katherine Hepburn, Lillian Hellman, Dashiell Hammett, and Golda Meir. Yet to me his most striking friendship of all, the one that made the deepest impression on me as a child, was the one he'd shared with the infamous Rosenbergs, Julius and Ethel, whom I'd heard about at school.

My grandfather was still living in Paris the year the Rosenbergs were convicted of conspiracy to commit espionage and sentenced to death, and the anger and helplessness he'd felt had proven more than he could bear. The day the couple was executed, June 19, 1953, only weeks after the death of Stalin himself, a neighbor had found my grandfather collapsed on the stairs in his building and had had him rushed to a nearby hospital where he'd lain insensible for nearly a week before recovering enough of his strength to return to his apartment, only to sit helpless and mumbling in a chair.

According to my mother, my father had met the Rosenbergs on a number of occasions when he was in college. He'd remembered his parents inviting the couple to their apartment for drinks and dinner one night, and the time, one scorching late July, when the two families had fled the city together for the Catskills where they'd rented adjacent bungalows at Kutsher's Hotel.

Yet, as I'd learned from my mother, their association had been even closer than that. On the evening the couple was executed at Sing Sing, my grandmother had taken my father to see the young Rosenberg boys, Michael and Robert, where they were staying with mutual friends, in hiding from the press, in a little house near Toms River, New Jersey. She'd insisted that my father dig out his old train set with which to distract the boys until they were safely tucked in their beds. This much is true, though my father claimed to remember it only vaguely—the framed pictures on the piano, the empty coat rack by the door. What he remembered clearly was the sound of the little train going round on its track and the new cowboy pajamas—clearly a gift from someone—that the youngest boy, Robert, had been wearing that night.

It is this, these details, that I inherited from my father and made my own, if with little means to interpret them, so that for years I dreamt them all: the empty coat rack, the tooting train, the new pajamas with their six-guns, cattle brands, and boots. I heard the traffic on the avenue; felt the sticky New York air; and saw Ethel, the boys' mother, as she was strapped into the chair. Yet there was more to it, more to my dreams than that, for while Julius Rosenberg had died after the first series of electrocutions, his wife Ethel had not, requiring two additional courses to finally stop her heart, a torment so violent, so grisly, that witnesses claim the muscles in her neck had bulged like tumors and wisps of smoke had risen from her head. Even now on occasion I am visited by the dream, startled from sleep by the image of my father kneeling on the floor with the Rosenberg boys, the toy train going round on its track, the smoke of skin and hair like a crown on Ethel's head.

His ears throb, his nose twitches, his senses now errant, irate: Someone in the building is masturbating, someone eating grapes!

His son David is rummaging around in his study. He

hears him from where he dozes in his chair on the lanai, hears the riffling of paper, the swollen-dry scraping of drawers. Then the clickety-clack of his old typewriter! a sound that burrows its way so quickly out of the folds of his brain that he hasn't the time to master his reaction, to stem the muddy torrent of feelings, the indignation, self-pity, and shame, rising above his chair like an avenging Angelus Novus to obliterate the world around him.

For such are his powers now, such his predicament: nothing escapes his eye, no mouse in the cupboard, no needle in the haystack, no self-abasing, self-negating lie. All is in cinders, all but that which he graces with the irony of his smile: a child here, a seagull there, a bicycle by the side of a road. He soars backwards and forwards though time, shrieking his terrible cry above the smoke and ashes of Vladivostok until his wings are in tatters, his penis stiff, and the only soft place that remains in the world is the plump and priggish vulva of his neighbor, Mrs. Katz, who sits all day before the television in her nightgown and curlers, following the strikes and blind stratagems of the war in Iraq, so that when he does come, when at last he lets himself into her apartment and lifts her dainty hem, she'll have something pat to say.

Yellowcake, hah! He'd once said that to her, just as the elevator door was closing, and ever since she has longed to rebut him, his ugly little Sonya, has longed to have her cake and eat it too. Such patience, forbearance! Such holy resignation: Well, what can we do? We must go on living! We shall go on living, Uncle Vanya! he cries aloud from his chair now, hoping that Mrs. Katz can hear him through the wall, hear how well he knows her mind, knows the stalwart clinking of her heart. For there are secrets he could tell: Trotsky hated peasants (icons and cockroaches), Dostoevsky Jews, though the point is something else, he suspects, biting his lip until it bleeds, something to do with his son, David, if not particular to him, to this particular time and place, something bright and elliptical, something arching (he sees cupolas, seashells, domes), though it hurts his head to think of it, blinds without light his parched and sallow eyes. Papers flutter round him like leaves and he wants to strike the boy down (Cossack! Vandal! Hun!), to defend what little is left of his own yet-earthly claim, but his muscles refuse to contend, slack and seditious where he sits, so that all he can do is listen, listen hard, shedding arms and legs, shedding, like skin, like scales, his kidneys, eyes, and teeth, until he is nothing (nothing?) but a large Allonautilus ear.

Time collapses, a heap: he hears the staggered heartbeats, the creaking of Spassky's chair, hears like a sneer the infernal hissing of the television cameras in their makeshift burlap wraps. He hears it all and frets (What is Bobby doing?), hears it all, hypothecates, tries to render in pictures the secret, septic sounds. He sees the board between them, the serried pieces—that knight to c3! He remembers the date, the day, sees the board and boggles (...17 QB-K3! 18 BxQ, KBxB)!, sees the chess board and cheers: But a child, the chutzpah! "The filthy, lying bastard people!" And there—so poignant—Byrne's glum and helpless queen...

The crates of paperbacks are the first things to go. Setting them in the hallway outside the front door, I am disappointed to see that no one—no curious neighbor or workman—has touched the odds and ends I'd left for the taking last night, the three large boxes in which I'd packed the last of my parent's pots and pans, their coffee cups, plates, and bowls. Only later that evening, while drowsing on the couch, had it occurred to me to affix a sign to the boxes inviting the neighbors to help themselves to the contents, for they are as a whole a strange and timorous lot, eyeing me suspiciously through their venetian blinds, each time I come and go, and averting their shrunken faces when I pass them in the hall.

I am due back in El Paso on Thursday to meet with the structural engineers about my latest project and, after hauling two more boxes to the hallway, take a break to check my e-mail before quickly reviewing the latest axonometric projections of the plan.

I cannot help but admire the design, its stark, aboriginal genius. After months of wrestling with different schemes and configurations, with radials, diamonds, pinwheels, T's, and K's, I'd finally hit upon the shape by chance one day while watching a television documentary on the ancient Nazca Lines of Peru. Of the many giant forms and figures carved into the Peruvian desert floor, there was one in particular that had caught my eye—a small unicursal labyrinth, the black and white photograph of which had been taken from an airplane just after the war by the late German mathematician Maria Reiche when she first began to study the glyphs. Alternately described as a "flower" and a "key," and by the unassuming Reiche herself as a "Spiral-ähnliche Figur," it was the very design I'd been searching for since I'd first sketched a proposal for the project that spring.

Obsessed with the vision, often unable to sleep, I'd visited the site, deep in the arid boot-heel of New Mexico, on three separate occasions when the firm was first bidding for the job, even interrupting my work in Bucharest to fly back out there, determined as I'd been to devise a plan I could sell. Yet each time I'd found myself lulled into submission by the miles and miles of open desert, by the blistering heat and haggard bearding of scrub brush and cacti. For there was little there upon which the untrained eye could rest, so that the brain tired easily, each bristling thought polished smooth as a stone.

At first I'd insisted upon wandering the site alone, so as to get a feeling for the land, threading my way through the tarbush and mesquite, punctuated here and there by the spiky, witch-like fingers of ocotillo, and wandering the wide, dry arroyo that cuts like scar across one corner of the enormous tract. To my delight I'd seen a banded gecko and some velvet ants, which I'd crouched to examine as they went about their work; and though I'd hoped to see a rattlesnake or scorpion I'd had no such luck.

I was there one afternoon when the summer rains came, flooding the wide dry arroyo in minutes, overturning one of our jeeps, and washing out the road by which the workmen had come. And then it was over: the clouds and moisture vanished—guzzled by the earth, sapped by the sun. Yet there was no mistaking the change. Suddenly the desert was alive with insects, lizards, and snakes; flowers bloomed, the air thick with the bitter-sweet stench of creosote bush, the olive-green scrub that covers the washes and bajadas for as far as the eye can see.

The site, just a stone's throw from the Mexican border, is located about twenty miles southeast of Big Hatchet Peak near an abandoned ranch town called McFarlands. Back in New York I'd studied the plot on my computer before my first trip to see it, unable as I'd been to grasp its dimensions. With the aid of topographical maps and satellite photos, I'd examined every square foot of the terrain and had been amazed at my inability to discover even a trace of human habitation there, no sign—neither roads nor ruins—of the original homesteaders and their efforts to eke out a living from the all but barren land.

The majority of the boot-heel is now in private hands, snatched up in the '80s by wealthy Texas ranchers and fenced off with barbed wire for no other purpose than to lay their claim on it, though only the occasional footsore Mexican would ever know it. So remote is the region that I am flown into the site by helicopter each morning and back out again each night, back to my hotel in El Paso, so that after a long and dusty day of work I can enjoy a hot shower, a good meal, and a plush queen-sized bed.

In my many weeks on the job there I've grown accustomed to my room at The Imperial, a proud if gloomy old hotel that has played host over the years to such lions and luminaries as Amelia Erhardt, Will Rogers, John Reed, Gloria Swanson, Eleanor Roosevelt, and Enrico Caruso. It is said that during the Mexican Revolution it was popular among the wealthier citizens of El Paso to watch the firefights between the revolutionaries and the Mexican Army from the hotel's rooftop terrace where I often sit for a drink after work. The waiters know me there, young Mexicans mostly who like to banter with me in Spanish, when I'm not too tired, talking of soccer and teasing me for my thick Castilian lisp.

From there, out beyond the fortified river with its spotlights and concertina wire, I can take in the full sweep of Ciudad Juárez, from its colorful market and baroque cathedral to the sprawling colonias at the base of the mountain where the poor and the wretched live. Further east I can make out the sulfur-colored lights of the maquiladoras, the many makeshift factories that line the border for miles, their legions of workers assembling goods—once shoes and blue jeans, now mostly electronics—for their ready exportation north.

While El Paso enjoys its status as one of the safest cities in the U.S., Ciudad Juárez, just across the river, has become a battleground for competing drug cartels, giving me, as I stand nursing a drink at the railing some nights, the strange, vertiginous feeling of a child at an aquarium gazing down upon a tank of hungry sharks. So far this year more than 1,800 people have been killed in the drug wars there alone, many of them women, the bodies often dismembered or otherwise mutilated beyond recognition, distinguishing the once-charming "Gateway to the North" as the single most murderous city on earth. Just last week I read a story in the *El Paso Times* that the Border Patrol had discovered the body of a man, pinned to the fence on the U.S. side, whose head had been replaced by that of a pig, stitched meticulously to the skin.

The first time I saw the stream of day-workers—nannies, cooks, and gardeners—filing back across the river to Mexico over the Stanton Street Bridge, it had reminded me of other fault lines around the world, of Jerusalem and Berlin, and of Johannesburg, when at nightfall the city become white again, every black man, woman, and child required by law to return to the squalid townships in which they lived. Just as I had in Johannesburg, I'd suffered there, on the rooftop terrace in El Paso that first night, the distinct, if hallucinatory impression that I was witnessing some sublime if redoubtable dance, the simple violence of which threatened to rend the world to bits if I so much as flinched. And I remember feeling, as I'd watched the workers filing slowly back across the bridge, that I myself was fine. Not safe, but fine, as if, for reasons still obscure to me, I'd been permitted a glimpse of something vast and malefic that defied my understanding then faded like a dream.

I was in my fifth and final year at Cooper Union when my mentor, an architect named Gilmour, invited me to join him on a trip to South Africa the following summer to consult with some developers on an innovative new prison he'd helped to design. While based in Johannesburg, we'd visited Durban and Cape Town, toured Kruger Park, and met with friends of his, South Africans, who'd owned a small farm in Swaziland. And just before our return to New York we'd spent a surreal if glorious week wandering the war-torn streets of Maputo, Mozambique, goggling at the matchless variety of crumbling Art Deco buildings wedged like Cubist flowers between drab, Soviet-style high-rises, while the battles raged around us in the hills, the sky at night illuminated by incendiary flares and rocket-propelled grenades.

I'd never seen so many homeless children as I'd seen

there, that week, refugees mostly from the villages up the coast. Each night, after the sun had set, the children had piled themselves one upon another for warmth before the large exhaust vents of the office buildings near the once-famous Café Continental where, following a dinner of vinho verde and peri-peri prawns, we'd often stopped for pastries and coffee before returning to our hotel.

By that time the Portuguese presence in the city was but a specter of its former self, the last of the colonists having fled the country en masse in the months before independence was declared. After more than four hundred years of brutal domination they'd vanished overnight, abandoning their villas, gardens, and clubs, and sabotaging much of the city's machinery, disabling cars and buses, contaminating the waterworks, and disrupting the power supply. From our hotel room we'd been able to see a gloomy cluster of unfinished high-rises, the empty elevator shafts of which—so the listless clerk had informed us one morning—the Portuguese developer had had filled in with cement before boarding one of the last flights out for Lisbon.

My mentor had introduced me to the hidden genius of 'generic cities', cities—largely developing world cities—that functioned well despite their apparent illogicality, their lack of formal planning. He'd loved the way that Maputo had already remade itself since the Portuguese exodus, and despite the civil war, overwhelming its stately avenues and gardens with its own essential scheme, the sidewalks, alleyways, and parking lots swallowed up, as overnight, by houses and restaurants, by markets and churches, by shops and schools and shebeens. He'd reveled in the daily tumult there, the din and confusion, determined, eager as he'd been, to develop a new, more organic urban architecture, one that took as its foundation not what a city might be but what it was in fact, what it yearned for, what it needed to be.

While working in El Paso I've often thought of him, my professor, of our time together in Maputo, of his lonely death from AIDS. I've often wondered what he'd have noticed—what I myself would have seen—had I toured that city with him.

Out of curiosity, as a means of passing the nights when I've returned to my room at The Imperial after a long day's work, too tired to sleep, too restless to watch the television, I've done some reading on the history of El Paso, bits and pieces from books and magazines, so that in the brief time since I started this job I've begun to recognize some of the city's deeper moods, each of which reminds me, if I am patient, that I am nowhere else but there. For El Paso is unlike any city I've known. Even the sounds there are different—the rumble of voices, the honking of cars, the steady drip-dripping in the large bathroom sink.

Once, one bright Sunday morning, when I was walking with my daughter Rachael and a friend of hers in Central Park, she'd asked me what El Paso was like, that city where I'd been spending so much time, and I found to my surprise that there was little I could tell her about the place, little I could say that would render it truly. For it is upon appearance an undeniably ugly place, a parched and barren crossroads of soldiers, gangsters, and priests, with few of the trappings one associates with the great cities of the world. Split by a spine of jagged, dun-colored mountains, there is an air of desperation in the streets, a mephitis of violence and greed, that she could never have seen, as I do, through the scrim of other, brighter things: the sharp dry heat, the lunchtime clatter of plates and glasses in the crowded tacquerias, the sing-song cries of parqueros, skinny, gap-toothed boys offering—at an extortionist's fee—to help you park your car.

From my corner room on the ninth floor I can see straight down El Paso Street to the border, just a few blocks away, and am often drawn to watch the street life there in the early mornings, before the shoppers and narcos emerge, pulling up a chair to the window and setting my breakfast on the ledge.

There is nothing remarkable about the street itself, about the shabby brick buildings, about the pawn shops and discount stores that clutter the sidewalks with their wares. What makes the scene compelling is simply its foreignness to me, for even the movements of the people there, as they pick through the handbags and shoes piled high in the bins before the shops, are somehow different to me, at once engrossing in their novelty and remarkably, decidedly obscure. If indeed all peoples are the same in the end, then they are differently so, animated in their blood and brains to such familiar behaviors as are practiced everywhere by genetically, even mythically different dreams, so that while one may well ascribe a surface conformity to the world—there, two young Mexican women are looking at jeans, holding them to their waists and laughing—the deepest motivations of a people may remain forever, ineluctably strange.

One day, feeling restless, I'd filed across the dry river amidst a throng of Taiwanese tourists, eager to visit the old cathedral, the buff-colored neoclassical towers of which I could see from my hotel window. Just over the bridge was Avenida Juárez, both sides of which were cluttered with curio shops, casas de cambio, and cut-rate pharmacies where the local gringos buy their prescriptions in bulk. I was told that the bars there, a few of which were already open, catered to college kids who crossed the bridge in packs each weekend to take advantage of the cheap women, tequila, and beer. In all of the shops I'd found the same goods for sale: serapes and sombreros, ceramics and glassware, leather goods, baskets, t-shirts, Mexican flags, and soccer jerseys, as well as the ubiquitous black velvet paintings of Villa, Zapata, and Che.

As instructed by my concierge, I'd followed the avenue until it intersected another avenue, one called 16th de Septiembre, where I'd turned right and continued on a half a dozen blocks to the Mercado Juárez, a warehouse-size building with fifty or sixty vendors selling the same cheap Mexican crafts and curios I had seen upon first crossing the bridge. There was a patio on one side there with a few restaurants, in one of which, empty but for an old woman sorting through some plastic bags, I'd sat for a beer in the shade of an umbrella, listening to the mariachis tuning up for the day before continuing on to Juárez Cathedral and the old Mission of Guadalupe. Surprised, if not disappointed by the modern interior of the cathedral, not knowing what it was I'd expected to find, what illumination or sign, I'd sat for a while on one of the pews in the hieratic dimness of the adjacent mission, all but stifled by the heat and silence there. Some school children had entered shortly after me, girls in blue pinafores, followed by a hunched old woman in black who'd knelt briefly at the altar, crossed herself three times, then struggled to her feet. Her rebozo—when she'd passed me—had smelled sweetly of smoke.

At last, feeling tired, discouraged, I'd retraced my steps back through the crowded streets and across the bridge to El Paso.

I AM CARRYING MY FATHER'S suits out to the hallway when I notice that the Saavedra's door is ajar. No one in the building ever leaves their door ajar and I cannot resist the idea that Melina is back, that she is here again to see her mother. And suddenly my heart is racing, my mouth is dry. Without thinking I tiptoe closer to the door, trying to get a glimpse inside, when a clatter of dishes sends me scurrying back to my father's place where I duck inside to collect myself.

Maria and Carlos Saavedra had been the first people to welcome my parents to the building, and for a time the four of them had been the fastest of friends, dining together at the club and playing bridge and gin rummy in the Saavedra's bright kitchen. Then my father and Carlos had had a falling out over Castro, and the relationship—for all my mother's efforts to save it—had cooled significantly, until, by the time of her death, the couples were no longer speaking at all.

I'd met the Saavedras on a number of occasions and had found them charming people—Carlos with his pressed white shirts, porkpie hat, and pencil-thin mustache; Maria with her ivory skin and slender, belted waist. Once while chatting with Maria in the foyer of their apartment while I was down visiting my parents, I'd noticed on the wall behind her a photograph of a young woman, a pretty girl with jet-black hair astride an old bicycle, her face ablaze with the surly, impudent sort of grin that has always thrilled me in women. When I'd asked my mother about the girl she'd supposed it was a niece or some cousin back in Cuba, as the Saavedras had never mentioned a child of their own.

It was not until years later, shortly after my mother's death, when I'd flown down to spend a couple of days with my father, that I'd met the girl herself, then a beautiful woman, the Saavedra's only child, Melina Villegas. I'd recognized her at once—the bright eyes, the grin—as I'd helped her into the elevator with her overloaded bags. She'd just done some grocery shopping for her mother, she'd explained to me, as she'd rummaged around in the tiny purse suspended by a strap from her faintly freckled shoulder. I'd taken the bags from her so that she could retrieve her keys, which she'd managed to do at once, holding them aloft for me with a grateful jingle. And I remember her scent as she'd pressed close me to make room for another couple that had entered the car behind us, a pleasant compounding of perfume, sunscreen, and perspiration that had reminded of me of lonely summers past.

She was wearing a light Indian print dress with a pair of finely tooled leather sandals that day, an outfit that had leant her a simple elegance sadly out of keeping with the ugly, shrimp-colored building with its mildewed walls and peeling paint. Scarcely arrived, she seemed impatient, eager to get away.

Which floor, she'd inquired of me, peering over the top of her sunglasses at the buttons by the door, and had been surprised to learn that I was going her way. Eager to explain, I'd told her that I knew her mother, had known her for years, at which point she'd wrinkled her flawless brow at me, her eyes flashing darkly over her sunglasses as though I'd just trumped her in a game she'd never expected to play. You know my mother? she'd said. Yes, your father, too. They were friends of my parents—the Anskys across the hall. The Anskys, she'd repeated softly, uncertainly, searching her memory for the name, and for a moment she'd looked so troubled I'd moved to reassure her. I'm David, I'd told her, juggling the bags to shake her hand. David? Yes, David Ansky. Nice to meet you, David. I'm Melina, she'd said.

She'd been named by her late father (so I'd learned that same evening when she'd asked me into their apartment for a drink) after the popular Greek actress and singer, Melina Mercouri. Her mother had gone to bed and we were sitting together on the balcony enjoying the pleasant clinking of halyards in the marina below, when, without prompting, she'd told me of her father's many and tumultuous affairs, and of the proud and silent way her mother had suffered the man, preparing his meals for him and ironing his fine white shirts. She herself had had dreams of poisoning him, of lacing his food with arsenic just to release her mother from his grip. For she'd often imagined her mother happy, pictured her laughing and dancing with friends.

But she'd been wrong about that, she'd confessed to me that evening, suddenly, affectingly demure. On the morning her father collapsed of a heart attack while tying his shoes her mother's spirit had fled the place with him. Since then, her mother had rarely left the apartment except to get her prescriptions filled, haunting the darkly decorated rooms with a presence so faint it was often difficult to detect it, but for the wraith-like jingling of the bracelets at her wrists.

For it was something more than grief that her mother had suffered, Melina had explained to me that evening, as if still trying to put her finger on it, to give it features, a face. Grief her mother had known, had tended for years, but the death of her husband had come as something else, something sordid, obscene, something altogether more than she could bear. What in her mother's behavior had initially conformed to the typical stages of mourning, as outlined in every handbook on grief—the shock, denial, and anger— had simply never given way, she'd explained to me that evening, never ceded an inch of ground to the cultivation of fresh habits and routines, though more than two years had passed since she'd found her husband dead.

Of course there were more widows in the building than windows, Melina had joked to me in an effort to lighten the mood. They were everywhere one turned, golfing, swimming, playing tennis, and riding the bus to Miami once or twice a month to take in their favorite shows. But not her mother, she'd whispered with a hint of asperity. No. It was hard to understand her mother sometimes.

I'd been surprised to learn, that evening, that Melina was a widow living in Miami on her own. Her husband, a successful real estate broker, had died in a hang gliding accident in Rio three years before. Though they'd often talked of having children, they'd never actually tried.

That evening she'd seemed relieved by the chance to unburden herself to me, a stranger, speaking in detail about her father's affairs, and about the night he'd struck her in the face for daring to confront him. She'd told me how he'd cursed her and sent her away, so that, until he'd died, she'd had to meet her mother in secret. And, as if for the first time in years, she'd talked at length about herself.

She loved mussels, she'd told me, read women's letters, and dreamed of seeing the Taj Mahal. For a few years, while she was still in her twenties, she'd worked with a printmaker in Paris, an elderly man who'd been shot in the foot in the war, had briefly entertained the possibility of becoming an artist, then had waited tables with a girlfriend in Antwerp before moving to Marseilles where she'd shared an apartment with a handsome Algerian who'd managed a nightclub there.

When pressed, she'd told me she now worked at the University of Miami, as the Production Supervisor for the medical school's monthly magazine, a job for which she was well-paid if often overworked. She'd taken the position shortly after her husband's death, and for a brief period it had helped to distract her, though it had left her little time for a private life, little time for family and friends. She was generally so tired after work she rarely went out at all, except for a run on the beach.

It wasn't a question of money. Her husband had left her financially secure, with a diverse portfolio of investments and a spacious high-rise apartment in South Beach over-looking the ocean and bay, so that if she chose to she could afford to spend her days there just enjoying the view. And I remember her saying—in what context I cannot recall— that she was deathly afraid of bats.

At one point, in the midst of telling me about a friend

of hers who had recently moved to Singapore, she'd interrupted herself to say, "So what happened with your wife?"

I'd been stymied by the question, having never mentioned Gina, but in passing, so that it had taken me a moment to gather my thoughts. "I suppose lots of things," I'd managed at length, not wanting to seem evasive, though I'd had nothing more to say. A man had appeared on the dock below us and, dark as it was, I'd watched him fiddle with the rigging of his boat before ducking inside the cabin. "Lots of things," I'd repeated, after a spell, hoping in that way to picture the matter more clearly, but could only shake my head. For, since my mother's death, I'd not spoken to anyone about Gina, so that the very subject seemed strange.

Yet Melina had been quick to reassure me. "Never mind," she'd said. "I'm sorry I asked. It's really none of my business."

"No, that's not it. Honestly. We were just…we were always just so busy," I'd struggled to explain, when for a moment I'd looked at her without speaking. "At first, after my daughter was born, I'd hardly travelled at all. I'd liked being home, playing games with Rachael, and spending the evenings watching television with my wife. On winter weekends I'd made pancakes and bacon after which we'd bundled ourselves up and made tracks through the snow. Whenever it had snowed we'd made a point of getting out early to be the first ones in the park, so that it was as if we'd wandered by accident into some dark, enchanted wood, holding hands and whistling away the wolves that flitted through the trees until the sun came up and the park was filled with people, when we'd hurried our way back home."

"And then? What changed?"

"I suppose I did," I'd said, amazed. I remember gazing at my hands. "I'd joined a new firm, had started travelling more, and eventually nothing between us was the same."

It was at that moment, as we were sitting there on the balcony, sipping sherry, the dark-bottled dregs of which she'd discovered in her mother's sideboard, that Melina had startled me by clutching my arm in what at first had seemed like a gesture of dread, as of some ghastly vision seen, only to soften at once, her fingers spreading themselves out upon the back of my hand with a yearning so palpable it had made me catch my breath. I hadn't said a word, only followed her back inside, past her mother's door, to the little bedroom where she slept. I remember the warmth of her neck, the firmness of her small brown breasts. Her pubic hair, dark as the hair on her head, had been shaved to a slender V.

At the time I was still living with my wife and daughter in our Madison Avenue apartment, sleeping in the guestroom where I'd piled my things, my suits and ties and shoes. It had been a temporary arrangement until I'd found a place of my own, so that as I'd lain there in the darkness beside Melina, listening to her steady, whispering breaths, I'd felt no guilt for what I'd done, no remorse, only a sickness at heart that I'd never lie that way with Gina again.

When next I check, the Saavedra's door is closed and the disappointment I feel is so acute I wince, doubling over as if struck by a blow. For this there is no accounting, as it has been months since I've even thought of Melina, of her eyes, her breasts, her grin.

Arming myself with a stack of my father's old newspapers, I cross once more to the Saavedra's door with its artificial wreath leftover from some Christmas past, and pause for a moment to listen, but to no avail. Even holding my breath I am unable to detect any noise within. The door lock, I notice, has recently been replaced, as has the doorknob itself, when it occurs to me with a gasp that someone else is living there now, that the kindly Mrs. Saavedra is dead.

I am about to knock, so reckless do I feel, so desperate, suddenly, to speak with Melina, to see her face, to tell her how I feel, when Rachael startles me from behind. "Grandpa wants you," she declares with that suppressed impatience I've come to expect from her. She has just returned from the pool, her hair wet, a bright orange towel wrapped snugly about her waist. "Something about the television, he says."

"Thanks," I manage, still shaken by the thought that Mrs. Saavedra is dead, that I might never see Melina again. "Tell him I'll be right in."

The garbage chute is located at the end of the long, open-air hallway, in a small, windowless room, the waxy green floor of which is crowded with paper sacks of cans and bottles bound for recycling. Once more I think of knocking to see if Mrs. Saavedra is there, prepared, if necessary, to ask after her health, to tell her about my father, that he's to be leaving the building in the morning, only to suffer the same sharp thrill at the thought of finding Melina there. For suddenly, after having nearly forgotten her, she is all I can think of.

Impulsively now, with no idea what I'll say, I rap twice on the Saavedra's door but there is no reply. Whoever it was I'd heard in there before must have gone out, I suppose, at once disappointed and relieved, and resolve to try again later, after I've showered and changed my clothes.

My knocking has alerted the residents on the floor, sent a shiver through their ranks, so that the moment I turn around I am greeted by a fluttering of blinds. To my left a door clicks shut, but not before I catch a glimpse of my father's neighbor, the horse-faced Mrs. Katz.

I find my father asleep in his chair, head toppled to one side, a trail of spittle on his lightly whiskered chin. Rachael is in the bathroom so that I cannot ask her for the particulars about the TV, as it appears to be working fine. It is only when I try the remote control that I discover the problem, promptly replacing the batteries from the supply of them I'd discovered in the freezer this morning, each of them wrapped meticulously in foil.

I'd seen the large button remote control advertised in a magazine in New York and had ordered one for my father who I knew was having trouble with his eyes. At first he'd refused to use it, having not even removed it from the packaging by the next time I visited him, though once I'd made it ready for him he'd quickly warmed to the slender, much-simplified controls, even thanking me, in his typical fashion, with a pat on my arm.

Suddenly he snorts beside me, eyes pinched closed as if resisting the light.

The last time I was down here I'd tried telling him about the boy, having no idea how or if the words would ever take shape between us, knowing only that I needed to tell him, needed to try to describe what had happened with the boy before my father lost all awareness of me for good. I'd told him about the desert there, in New Mexico, about the men with their trucks and trailers. As he'd stared dumbly at me with his pale blue eyes, I'd told him about the heat and about the dust that rose in towering funnels around us as we worked, only to vanish in a flash, leaving the air so clear, so still, it seemed crystalline.

And I'd told him about the boy, about how I'd watched him die there, a Mexican boy, no more than eight or nine, who had lost his way in the scrub. I'd described for my father, feeling for the words as if my tongue itself were blind, the way the boy had appeared out of nowhere, materializing there beside the foreman's truck as if he'd dropped straight from the sky. But my father had made no reply to me, given no indication that he'd heard me at all, let alone grasped what I'd said, scratching his chin and finally closing his scaly eyes.

Now the pool is empty, my daughter showering, the women gone. Out beyond the rotunda the tennis courts are full, despite the heat, and for a moment I listen to the pleasant ponging of balls.

I have always liked the view from here, the emerald lawns, the eyebrow ponds, the curving palm-lined drive that brings one back on a spit of land through primeval stands of mangrove to the main road that links the city to the bay, San Carlos Bay, and to the new island causeway just visible beyond. There is something stirring to me in the flagrant artificiality of it all, a glimpse of perfection, of paradise, as tempting as it is appalling, absurd. Even time here seems suspended, as though a single day were a dozen days long. The very air disarms me, so that it requires but a matter of hours, after touching down here in Florida, before I begin to lose my sense of purpose and place.

Twice in the midst of the protracted annulment proceedings, I'd made the trip down here, not so much to see my father, who'd tended to ignore me, when he was conscious of me at all, but to get away from New York, from my work and friends, floating on my back in the pool late at night and sitting for hours in my mother's bedroom by the window in her favorite rattan chair.

I don't remember thinking much of anything at the time, as if suddenly I was no longer capable of initiating a world of my own, of thinking a thought, of making even a simple gesture, my limbs inert, my brain but a passive receptor of signals and signs, a static ground upon which other, sometimes darker forces played. I remember the clouds; I remember thinking that the clouds were somehow more than clouds, that they were somehow even more than my thinking that they were somehow more than clouds. I know that I didn't feel sad, only a little sorry for myself, the way I'd felt on occasion as a child when I'd been overlooked or forsaken by friends. Though many months had passed since I'd taken an apartment on my own, months in which I'd broken an ankle, spent three weeks alone at our house in Shelter Island, had an affair with a Finnish woman, and forgotten my daughter's fourteenth birthday, I'd simply been unable to accept the fact that Gina and I were through. I'd seen her everywhere I looked—in magazines, in passing cars, in the windows of familiar restaurants, shops, and bars. Just a laugh like hers in a crowded subway or a whiff of her perfume was enough to send me reeling for days.

Not even in Shelter Island, where we'd never bothered to know anyone, haunting the old house and nearby beaches each summer with the fickle felicity of tourists, had I been able to escape Gina's hold on me. January there was cold and rainy; I'd spent most of the time huddled inside, listening to the radio and watching the clouds gallop seaward. I'd read and slept; I'd drunk vodka in the kitchen, where it was warm, marking the arrivals and departures of the Greenport ferry through the dark and bleary panes. When the rain let up, as it occasionally had, I'd gone for breakfast at the little pharmacy in town, then stopped to study the gravestones in the old Quaker cemetery or wandered the Mashomack trails, there at the end of the world, gazing blindly at the birds.

For months after our separation I'd refused to consider the facts, to do what my mother had insisted I do, that is, stop feeling sorry for myself and take a long, hard look at what I'd done. For she'd been convinced—whatever Gina's faults—that I alone was to blame.

While here in Florida I'd thought a lot about Gina, about the way we'd met and fell in love one summer—photographs mostly, snapshots and impressions I still carry in my head of Utrecht and Amsterdam, between which we'd shuttled by sunlit train. I'd thought about the sex, the drugs, the hours we'd spent talking over coffee, one dark and rainy day, at the beautiful Kröller-Müller museum. And I'd thought about her dreams that summer, when we'd lain twisted together in bed, about the way she'd groaned and whimpered in her sleep.

That summer Gina had been awarded a Fulbright to study the Golden Age of Dutch art in Amsterdam, one of a dozen Americans with whom she'd lived in a converted hofje on Egelantierstraat. I'd happened to meet her one night at place called Café Nol. She'd asked me for the time.

At the time I was living with a friend in Utrecht, having nearly completed a program in architecture and urban design at an art school on Jodenbreesstraat, near the Rembrandt Museum, and was feeling so homesick that I'd instantly fallen for her brusque Jersey accent, the like of which I hadn't heard in years.

That first night I'd learned she was Italian, a Catholic, Sicilian, that she loved sushi, thought Rembrandt overrated. She'd had a weakness for expensive Dutch shoes, which she'd tried on for me in shop after shop, with no intention of buying, only to collapse beside me, giddy from exhaustion, in some backstreet cafe. She'd known a lot about art, I'd been impressed to learn—about Titian and Delacroix, about Balthus, de Kooning, and Johns. A graduate of Barnard, she was enrolled at Columbia when I met her, working on a Masters in Art History and hoping to find work that fall in some gallery or museum.

I'd never met anyone so determined, so tenacious in her will to wring the most out of every day, and used simply to watch her as she talked, amazed by her restless, hungry way of speaking, and by her moods, which had swept across her face with a violence that had often left me anxious, perplexed. One minute she might be telling me about the historic appearance of maps in the work of Vermeer or debating Clement Greenberg's definition of kitsch, clenching my hand where we sat by the canal near her house or wandered the crowded Vondelpark at dusk, when she would break off with a start, scowling at some thought or recollection, only to leave me without a word. For this she'd been quick to apologize, when next we'd met, kissing me hard and assuring me that her behavior had had nothing to with me.

Only slowly that summer had she begun to wonder about me, to wonder aloud, that is, pressing me steadily about my studies in Amsterdam, about my parents and my sister, and about my plans for the years to come. She'd often met me after class for an early dinner at one of the Indonesian restaurants I knew. It had seemed she was always hungry, devouring the pickled vegetables, skewered meats, and heaps of fried rice as though she hadn't eaten in days. And at her bidding I'd told her all about my classes there, so that soon I was dreaming aloud to her about my future as an architect, about the plans I'd envisioned, the innovations I'd make.

At the time I'd been under the spell of a particular instructor of mine, an acclaimed if controversial young architect named Simone Maes, who'd chosen to mentor me that year, sharing with me a number of her current projects and arranging for me to work as an intern that fall at a prestigious New York firm. Earlier that year she'd shown me one of her latest buildings, a home for the blind in Rotterdam that had transformed my thinking about architecture, had transformed my thinking about the blind. Built largely of chrome and glass, and shot throughout with green and purple walls, it had been conceived in violent opposition to every such institution she'd seen. Her design, once released, had created an uproar in the dissentious port city, the vision widely criticized as impractical and extravagant, as arrogant, reckless, profane. Yet she'd refused to submit to the pressure, even to compromise with her clients, declining to be interviewed while driving the project to completion, convinced as she'd been that even the blind deserved light. By the time she'd received what was to be the first of three international awards for her design I was back in New York. Thrilled by the news, I'd written her a letter but received no reply.

I'd told Gina all about her, and about my plans when I returned to New York, speaking about the future with a brazenness and conviction that had finally swayed her in the end. She'd told me so herself, some many years later, of how she'd fallen in love with me that day, her last in Amsterdam, when we'd met by the roses in the Begijnhof garden.

Here in Florida on my own, I'd thought a lot about that summer with Gina, about all that had happened since then. And I'd thought a lot about my father. Most nights he'd watched television on the lanai, brash, insipid comedies that had forced me to seek refuge in my mother's room, sipping bourbon in her chair by the window, neither thinking nor feeling, happy as a child to watch the cars streaming over the causeway to Sanibel Island where the lighthouse blinked its ancient warning.

Come daylight there wasn't much for me to do; sometimes I'd worked a bit on my laptop or ran errands for my father—brief forays to the liquor store or pharmacy, or to the nearest Winn-Dixie for his lottery tickets—anything to pass the time until I could clear my head. He didn't like it when I sat to watch the news with him, so that in the mornings after breakfast I'd often wandered the overgrown grounds, admiring the handsome boats in the marina and looking for alligators sunning themselves on the banks of the many well-stocked ponds. Some days, before it got too hot, I'd taken a spin on my mother's old bike. She'd kept a bright pink bicycle with a basket and tassels that I'd pedaled along the paths between the great banyan trees before it got too hot, indifferent to the residents and tourists who'd stopped to look at me and laugh.

My mother had loved to ride bikes. Back in Ithaca we'd often roamed the university campus together on our sturdy old Schwinns, my mother pumping away behind me with her bright, tinny bell as I blazed a trail through the hordes of students and professors that swallowed up the footpaths between classes. Setting out from McGraw Hall in Old Stone Row, where my father had had his office, we'd liked to loop down around Sage Chapel and the Statler Hotel to Minn's Garden and the Summer House before making the lazy circuit of Beebe Lake, if it wasn't too windy, by way of the Sackett Foot Bridge.

It was my mother who had shown me the sarcophagi in Sage Chapel. There, beneath the Gothic windows, with their Tiffany glass saints, was a life-sized marble effigy of the founder and first president of the university, Ezra Cornell, as well as the stirring likeness of a woman named Jenny McGraw Fiske, a simulacrum so real it had haunted me for days. Indeed often, after my mother had taken me there, after she had shown me that the doors were kept unlocked, that one might enter the place at will, without occasion at all, I'd ventured there on my own to admire the coolly recumbent woman, amazed by her lifelike detail, by her bold if stagnant beauty, stroking the fancy stitch-work and tassels of the pillow beneath her head and trying with my fingers to distinguish her toes beneath the wrinkled marble sheet. It was the very way I was to think of my mother once she died—so calm, so beautiful in death.

When I think of Cornell it is my mother I see, for it was with her, through her, that I'd come to know the place best. I remember pretending I was sick in order to spend the day with her in her favorite carrel in the library while she worked on her dissertation. I'd had to promise to be quiet, to get up and wander around the moment I felt restless, which I often had, pulling books from the shelves at random, and staring out the windows at the naked black trees.

She was writing about the work of an author with the unlikely name of Ford Maddox Ford. I remember asking her about the man and about the title of her study, *Women and Deception in the Work of Ford Maddox Ford*, and I remember the funny way she'd wrinkled her nose at me, mussing my hair and sending me on my way. The fact that she herself was having an affair at the time would have been inconceivable to me then, not because I'd idealized her marriage to my father, for I'd long preferred her without him, nor because I'd believed her incapable of such deception, such needs, though the thought of her behaving imprudently had never crossed my mind. It would have been beyond my capacity to imagine it then simply because she was still for me, as my mother, little more than a lively projection of my needs. Then my conception of her was largely subjective, so that it would have surprised me to learn that she had a life of her own.

Yet in looking back it is an altogether different matter: in retrospect her affair with Michael Radetsky makes a certain plain sense to me, in the way that events, even regrettable ones, have a way of seeming obvious, even fated, once they're past. Things happen as they do; it is perhaps the only truth that matters.

I was with my mother the time she first cut Michael's hair. I don't recall anything unusual or untoward about the occasion, except perhaps for the teasing admiration she'd expressed for his thick black curls. She'd enjoyed cutting people's hair, when she'd had the time, usually at the table in the yard over a glass or two of wine. She'd once cut Mr. Rabinovich's hair, trimming it the way he'd liked it, but not before nicking one of his large red ears, a simple mishap which he'd shrugged off with a winsome chuckle, dabbing at the wound with the corner of a napkin that he'd dipped in his beer.

The day my mother cut Michael's hair she'd brought me along with her; he'd asked her to do some typing for him and must have suggested that she bring her scissors as well, for she'd had them with her when we climbed from the car.

We'd found Michael tending his goats out back of his house where he'd planted a garden of carrots and spinach and peas, which he'd fenced off with chicken wire. A city boy, he was proud of the little garden, and my mother had flattered him to tell us about it, which he'd done in fine detail, leading us along the freshly turned rows and rejoicing like a child at every green sprout.

The old farmhouse house had really taken shape in the months since he'd purchased it. He'd surprised himself by building shelves and cupboards and a dark rustic table with knotty benches that was long enough, he'd boasted, to accommodate Jesus and all his Apostles on a single side.

He'd even repaired the plumbing so that the pipes no longer screeched.

It was hot that day that my mother cut his hair on the porch, moving deftly about him in her cut-off shorts and halter-top to the sound of one of Michael's records. I remember she'd chattered restlessly about my father, about his moods and his insomnia, and about her dissertation in terms I'd found difficult to follow, all the while sipping wine from a cracked china cup.

She'd cut Michael's hair too short, as he'd made clear by his expression when he'd finally considered himself in her handheld mirror, though he'd been too polite, perhaps too smitten, to say so, thanking her simply with a kiss on the cheek. Then for a while they'd disappeared inside, so that I'd been left to wander around the yard, chucking rocks at the mailbox and watching the chickens as they rooted through the grass that grew in patches beneath the old apple trees.

I could see a slice of the lake from there and a spattering of tiny white sails that might have been dabs on a canvas for the little they moved. Not a car passed on the narrow two-lane road that wound its way up the hill from town, and for a spell I'd amused myself by imagining the road in earlier days, when it wasn't a road at all and Indians—the Onondagas and Cayugas—were everywhere afoot.

By the time my mother and Michael returned outside I'd fallen asleep in the hammock strung laxly between two pines at the top of the rutted drive. The music had stopped and I remember, just before we'd left, spotting a lock of Michael's hair on the crooked front steps.

THAT SUMMER MICHAEL RADETSKY HAD been a frequent guest in our home; as his garden grew in he'd appeared at our house, once, sometimes twice a week, with a basketful of vegetables, which he'd cleaned and chopped for my mother in the kitchen while she cooked, the radio playing loudly, the back door opened wide.

Initially he and my father had gotten on well, Michael ever willing to play the novitiate to him, listening, smiling, and nodding his curly head, when in retrospect it is clear to me that, even then, as he'd enjoyed my father's food and drank my father's wine where they'd sat talking together on the sagging front porch, looking out down the long dark lane of elms, even then he must have felt in his heart an unalloyed contempt for the pale, bespectacled man with his ratty tweed jackets and sesquipedalian talk of "anti-humanism" and "theoretical practice," must have seethed with disgust at the tidy trappings of our handsome bourgeois home. Sitting there in the thickly fallen night, he must have cursed every cracked and fallen god that a man like my father could have won himself such a bright and fetching young wife.

For it had been plain to me, even then, that Michael was in love.

I remember he'd liked to do simple sketches of my mother with a charcoal pencil, capturing her here in the yard in a loose print dress and wide straw hat, there in the front parlor in one of the ugly chintz chairs left over from the days when the house was a small hotel. To win my favor he'd often brought me gifts when he'd stopped by to see us—comic books, arrowheads, and baseball cards, and had once surprised me with the hand-painted shell of a horse-shoe crab, which, for want of a clear purpose, I'd hung from a nail by my door.

As a contrast to my father I'd liked him very much. I'd liked the way he'd played checkers with my sister and me, the way he'd listened to my mother without interrupting her, the way, without thinking, he'd stroked my head when he was tired.

Recently, his book on industrial slavery in the American South had been purchased by a respected New York publisher, much to my father's chagrin, and, though the news was celebrated wherever Michael turned that summer, he himself was wretched, mooning about our kitchen as though his dog had just died, only to retreat to his house on the hill, after which we hadn't seen him for days. As a child I'd scarcely noticed his absence, except perhaps obliquely, in my mother's changing moods.

It was not for lack of feeling that I'd never wondered about Michael's depression, for I'd often enjoyed his presence in our house. I was simply happy to take the world for granted—pleased by appearances, persuaded in full by the surface of things. Adult life for me then was largely a matter of symptoms, a simple tally of what I saw and heard, and while I might have read more deeply into the daily bearing of my parents and of Michael Radetsky, marking their habits, connecting this with that, there was little reason for me to do so, so long as I myself was content.

It was only when I too was made to feel the sting of their relations that I considered the matter more deeply, as when my parents argued or when my mother despaired openly for

Michael's health, as she had for one long summer, moping around the house and muttering strangely to herself as though I wasn't even there.

For one day an assistant of Michael's, a girl I'd often seen on campus, had found him collapsed on his kitchen floor and had had him rushed to the hospital where they'd pumped his stomach and treated him for dehydration. Apparently, he'd swallowed a bottle of pills. All of this I'd learned only much later, after my parents had separated and my mother was living on her own in New York. She'd taken me to dinner at a little Indian restaurant on Broadway, where, in a dark corner booth beneath a gaudy painting of Ganesh, she'd told me about her affair with Michael Radestsky, even then so long ago. Naturally, I'd assumed that Michael's suicide attempt had had something to do with her, but she'd been quick to disabuse me of the notion, stating plainly, between sips of wine, that Michael Radetsky would never have killed himself for love.

Politics had been his only true passion, she'd told me in the restaurant that evening, with no intention of being dramatic. A child in Greenwich Village in the 1950's, Michael had grown up steeped in the spirit of the times, singing union songs, attending marches, and participating in the annual May Day festivities in Washington Square Park. His education had been typical of progressive New York Jews—the Little Red Schoolhouse and then Elizabeth Irwin High, where he'd distinguished himself in writing and debate. He'd traveled widely in Europe with his family, attended lectures at the New School, visited museums, and studied violin. And he'd prided himself on his many black and Puerto Rican friends.

Still his childhood, like my father's, had not been an easy one. "By the early '50s the Russians had exploded their first atomic bomb," my mother had explained, in her effort to untangle Michael's character for me. "The Korean War had begun and American anti-Communist fever was rampant. Hundreds of Americans were sent to prison, thousands lost their jobs, and many more were bullied into silence, exile or betrayal by Senator McCarthy and his televised witch-hunts. For a whole year Michael's father, under suspicion for his association with a former Marxist colleague at NYU, had been barred from entering his classroom, so that he'd been forced to wait tables at a Greek restaurant there on MacDougal Street to pay the monthly bills."

It was out of that charged and volatile milieu that Michael Radetsky had emerged at Cornell in the fall of '69. By then he was both a committed activist and an ambitious young historian whose specialty, American slavery, was in itself a political act. And it was there, in his chosen field of study, that his politics had diverged most sharply from my father's, a fellow historian and former radical just thirteen years his senior. Since the assassinations of King and Malcolm X, Michael, like many other young radicals, had grown disillusioned with the talk of patience, non-violence, and restraint, with the weary maxims of men like my father, drawn instead, like a moth to flame, to the militant Marxism of the newly emergent Black Panthers, even traveling by bus that November to attend a Black Panther Constitutional Convention in Philadelphia.

"It was about that time that they'd parted ways," my mother had told me that evening, helping herself to more wine. "Your father would have none of Michael's aggressive posturing, prodding him, baiting him over the chess board, each time they'd met, until Michael erupted in rage." For, as my mother had explained it to me, my father had touched a nerve in Michael, touched it, then rubbed it raw.

Not only was Michael white at a time when the Black Panthers wanted nothing to do with white people, but as an associate professor at Cornell he was part of the very system, the very establishment, the Panthers were seeking to overthrow. Months passed with Michael growing every day more silent and morose, and for a time we hardly saw him at all. "Then one day," my mother had explained, "after weeks of steady rain and mounting political tension on campus, there came the opportunity Michael had been waiting for, the chance to show his true colors at last."

Under pressure from black students, the administration at Cornell had finally agreed to offer a colloquium on Black History, to the hasty preparation of which Michael had devoted himself with a passion he hadn't felt in years. Torn as he'd been between his increasingly radical activism and his budding academic career, the new course promised him the opportunity to reconcile his teaching and politics without compromising either. Yet the course had not come off as planned.

"You see, the black students took issue with Michael at once, claiming that all history was the history of whites versus blacks, all history the history of the struggle of the black race against its white oppressor, and that therefore they could never accept any research or interpretation by a white man. They'd heckled him daily, poor man, refusing to read or write, so that by the third week of class not a single black student remained, a rejection of both Michael and his work that had devastated him and from which it had seemed unlikely he'd recover."

But recover he had; once released from the hospital he'd seemed a changed man. The storm in his eyes had passed and soon they'd regained their mischievous sparkle. Each day he'd woken early, fed his goats and chickens, then written for a couple of hours before class. With his white students he was more popular than ever and spent many hours meeting with them between classes to talk about their work. And for the first time since he'd moved to Ithaca he'd found himself a girlfriend, a pretty waitress and part-time graduate student named Clarice.

At first jealous of her, my mother had sat with her books and papers in the popular diner where Michael's new girlfriend had worked, studying the woman as she'd chatted with her customers and trying to imagine her and Michael in bed. Yet it wasn't the sex that had troubled her. "No, it wasn't the sex at all," she'd explained to me that evening. There'd been something else about Michael that had held her fast to him, a nearly desperate sense of purpose that she'd felt as an aching in her chest even then. "For he genuinely believed in things, David," she'd insisted, in a voice so harrowed with feeling that I'd nearly touched her hand. "Incredible as it seems, he believed in Truth, in Truth and Justice, in the very History that unmade him in the end. He believed that the Good Fight was well worth fighting."

By that time the waiter had brought us our check. It was late and we'd stumbled our way out into the watery light of

Broadway where my mother had kissed me on the cheek. She'd told me she was pleased to have had the chance to talk with me a bit, to tell me about Michael Radetsky, and had promised to tell me more about him in the future.

We never did meet to talk about Michael again, though I did in fact learn more about him, about the final year of his life, when I'd chanced upon a reference to him in a book review in *The New York Times*. Without even finishing the review I'd rushed out to the local bookstore and purchased a copy of the book, a conservative critique of the role of young Jews in the radical Left. It was from there that I'd learned the details of his suicide, that I'd read about his ties to the Weather Underground and about the large cache of weapons he'd amassed in his house.

By then my mother was dying of cancer in Florida and though I'd mentioned the book to her, mentioned Michael himself, she'd seemed too bleary to understand me, as if trapped between consciousness and sleep. It was just as I was preparing to leave—for I'd been at her bedside all day, reading to her and holding her hand—that she'd whispered: "You know, he called me on the telephone that night."

"Which night?" I'd pressed her, certain she was speaking of Michael Radetsky, of the night he'd killed himself, but she didn't appear to have heard me, her face thin and white, her eyes fixed hard upon a spot above my head. Such, I'd guessed, was the effect of the morphine.

"He was clearly upset. I think he'd been crying. He kept talking about how he couldn't write anymore and how the icy roads made him feel trapped in the house and how Cambodia was being bombed and nobody seemed to care."

There she'd paused to catch her raspy breath. "He'd brought his goats into the kitchen and he begged me to come over to cut his hair, but I refused, knowing where it would lead us and not trusting myself on the icy roads. That was the winter your father broke his hip...such snow that year... and by then...by that point, what more could I have said?" she'd stammered to me in the dimness of her room, at which point her words had dissolved into mumbling, so that I'd been unable to grasp them, her lips trembling mutely until the drugs overwhelmed her.

The final year of Michael Radetsky's life was a bleak and lonely one, as described in the brief account I'd read of it. By then he'd grown paranoid, convinced that the Black Panthers were trying to kill him and that the FBI was tracking his every move, so that he'd refused to use the telephone and rarely emerged from his tightly shuttered house except to teach his classes twice a week and to buy his groceries in town.

Then, that December, after months in isolation, he'd suddenly appeared on a panel of speakers at a much-publicized conference called 'The Black Man in America: 350 Years: 1619-1969' at Wayne State University.

A few of his colleagues had persuaded him to speak on the subject of slavery, which finally he'd agreed to do, hoping at last to prove his commitment to the struggle. His paper had been a seemingly straightforward analysis of the different levels of slave accommodation as revealed in the letters of slave drivers, managers, and house servants to their masters and mistresses. Well aware of the charged atmosphere in the room that day, he'd treaded lightly, chatting easily with his friend and fellow panelist, the historian

Eugene Genovese, in the crowded lobby, even sharing a few words with the other two participants who'd arrived on the stage just after the conference began, the prominent black nationalists, Sterling Stuckey and Julius Lester, whom he'd met before in D.C..

After Michael delivered his paper Eugene Genovese had been the first to respond. While he'd disagreed with Michael on a couple of key points, he'd remained well within the rules of conventional criticism, even praising Michael for his depiction of the hierarchy within the slave community itself. Sterling Stuckey, by contrast, had gone on the offensive at once, rereading the letters—the same letters that Michael had just used in his talk—in a starkly different voice, only to conclude by accusing Michael of having proposed nothing more than the same old Sambo thesis dressed up in sheep's clothes.

To this Michael might have managed a reply but Julius Lester, the third and final discussant, had broken in before he could speak. It was his reaction that had hit Michael the hardest, for the outspoken Lester had not even bothered to consider Michael's findings, his many years of meticulous research, but had launched a direct attack on the man himself.

"Who the hell are you to tell a black man anything about himself?" Lester had demanded of him "You with your pearly white skin and your fancy Ph.D.? The proper study for a white man is white history and white history alone. You wanna know about 'The Black Man in America'?" he'd clamored, rising to his feet and actually coming around the table to jab a finger in Michael's face. "I'll tell you about the black man in America. The black man in America is sick and tired of the white man in America telling him how to think and how to live and how to brush his goddamned teeth! You wanna know about the black man in America? Then listen to the black man himself! Listen to him now when he tells you he's got no need of your kind—not now, not ever!" he'd battered the unsuspecting Michael where he'd sat dumbstruck at the end of the table, rising only when the audience exploded in applause.

According to the author, it was that, Michael's humiliation at the conference in Detroit, that had finally broken him. At once, upon returning to Ithaca, he'd taken a leave of absence from his teaching, holing himself up in his house on the hill once more and refusing to answer the phone. It had been snowing for weeks and the drifts had piled up so high around the little house that the police and paramedics had had to shovel their way inside where they'd found him curled naked at the top of the stairs, skull shattered, nostrils black with blood.

Strangely, I have no memory of his death, though I've a vague recollection of driving by his house with my mother some many months later and seeing the apple trees in bloom. Angered, exhausted by the turmoil on campus, my father had taken to spending more time at home, working at the desk in his study, helping my mother in the garden, and sitting with my sister who'd never tired of the stories he'd read to her, those of Hans Christian Andersen and the Brothers Grimm, thick leather-bound editions of which he'd kept at the ready by his chair.

Michael's death in Ithaca that winter seemed to have burst the floodgates of time, so that the subsequent weeks, months, and years had passed in a blur. My sister Lily's hair had turned from blonde to brown, the fountain pump had quit one day and had never been replaced, and my mother had completed her dissertation to modest if general acclaim. I remember my parents had scarcely argued at all.

And I too had changed. In the blink of an eye I'd taken up drawing with a teacher in town, broken my arm while skating, learned to drive, fallen in and out of love with a girl named Maureen Frasier, and graduated with honors from the local high school. Only occasionally had I ever thought of Michael during that time, and then always with an uneasy feeling in my stomach that had made me long for the day when I would leave the town for good.

For by then I'd known I had to get away—from Ithaca, from my father. While my classmates also spoke of escaping, of joining the army or going to college, most of them stayed close to home after graduation, marrying local girls, fixing up houses in town, and taking up their father's jobs. Such was not an option for me.

In the meantime, I'd simply avoided my father, biding my time by reading and drawing and taking long drives around the lakes. My father never fully recovered from his broken hip that winter so that he'd been forced to hobble around the campus with a cane, and I remember thinking, shortly before I'd left for college that year, how very old he'd seemed.

He'd talked often of retirement then, soured as he'd been by the behavior of his students, who'd seemed to him every day more defiant, more fractious, scouring the classifieds each week in the hope of finding for himself and my mother a smaller, more suitable home. Yet even years later, after my sister too had left for college, he'd been reluctant to sell the old house, having grown deeply sentimental about the place, rewiring the sconces in the hallway and patiently refinishing the old Adam mantel in the den. Some days he'd sat for hours on the sagging front porch, just gazing at the trees.

At the suggestion of his doctor, he'd made a habit of hiking the broader trails along the gorge before breakfast each day as a way of exercising his hip and improving his circulation, which had never been good. The habit had restored his appetite so that when I'd first returned from college I'd found him at least ten pounds heavier, his eyes bright, his typically ashen skin a healthy, hearty pink. He'd been sailing every day, he'd told me proudly, before I could even greet my mother, seizing me by the arm and ushering me into his study where he'd produced for me, beneath the light on his desk, a photograph of himself standing proudly beside his small white boat. Of course he'd named her *The Natalya*. What else?

Caught off guard, confused by his affection, I'd agreed to rise early to go sailing with him the next morning. He'd liked the mornings best, when the breeze was from the South. It had rained all night so that the air was damp and clear and I remember how the mist had hung like ribbons along the shore.

We'd hardly spoken at all during my first year away at college, so that it was with trepidation that I'd clambered aboard the boat with him that day. I'd read the reviews of his book on Trotsky, all but one of them unfavorable, and knew from my mother how deeply he'd suffered them. Still there was little sign of his anguish that morning; freshly shaven, he'd whistled jauntily as he'd rigged out the boat, and soon we were puttering our way out of the marina.

It was clear he was still a novice sailor, though he'd done his best that morning to convince me otherwise, working the sails with a studied insouciance, distracting me with a host of seemingly arbitrary commands that had sent me scrambling back and forth across the narrow deck and doggedly whistling the same old tune. Still we'd had a pleasant sail that day, hugging the eastern shore until we'd reached the park at Myers Point before tacking across the lake and back down the other side to his slip at Johnson Boatyard where we'd chatted for a spell with some of the other day-sailors before climbing the hill back home.

At one point in our sailing, when temporarily the breeze had died out and it had felt as though we were hanging there, as by magic, above the bottom of the deep, dark lake, he'd informed me, perhaps as a way of making conversation, that my 8th grade math teacher Mrs. Velasquez had died the other day.

It was an odd thing for him to have shared with me, given that he'd rarely had anything to do with my schooling. As far as I knew he'd never met a single one of my teachers, never attended a PTA meeting, never even bothered to read my reports cards that my mother had placed before him, as a matter of course, at the end of each term. What had made his telling me about Mrs. Velasquez particularly strange was that he'd never done anything to protect me from this self-same woman who'd tormented me for the better part of a year, when I was a student in her class, berating me with her elliptical tirades against the "Red Chinese" for whom she'd made me—who'd cared nothing for politics—their sputtering and helpless proxy. Time and again she'd turned on me in the middle of a lesson to lecture me and my classmates on the many and insidious ways the Chinese were infiltrating and undermining our lives in America, numbing us with television, making us fat and lazy, and filling our veins with their drugs, with their heroin and cocaine, which they pedaled on playgrounds in every park and school. It had never occurred to me that she'd considered my father a "Red", that she'd imagined him, this pale and flaccid man who'd often sat for hours on the porch with a book face-down in his lap, as a traitor and malcontent, a Judas in our midst.

When I'd complained to him about Mrs. Velasquez one day, nearly beside myself with rage, he'd merely chuckled at the matter, dismissing her (as apparently he'd expected me to do) as "a silly old cow". Only my mother had paid me any mind when I'd complained to her about the implacable woman, agreeing, after I'd collapsed in tears at the dinner table one evening, to speak to Mrs. Velasquez the very next day. And so she had, asking me to wait for her on the bench outside the classroom until she was through.

I have no knowledge of what transpired between them that day, only that I was soon transferred to another class, a remedial section of the same course in which, for want of any real expectations, I'd floundered miserably, barely scraping by with a C.

"She died in her sleep," my father had informed me that morning on the boat. "I read it in the paper last week. Apparently she was fond of collecting—odd things, really: old tobacco tins and Depression glass. What do you make of that?"

At the time I'd had no idea how to respond to this trivia, no way of knowing how or even if I should reply. For my father had often spoken to me this way, when I was younger, casting facts at my feet like little stones, which I never knew whether to collect or ignore. Baffled, impatient, I'd said nothing that day, pretending I hadn't heard him, all the while hoping that he'd elaborate on the matter, that he'd explain his intentions to me.

Yet he'd said all he'd had to say on the matter, indeed appeared to have forgotten the subject altogether by the time we'd started back toward town, talking instead about the fishing on the lake as if we'd been talking about the fishing all day—about the bullheads and bass, and about the recent resurgence of the carnivorous northern pike.

I'd thought of telling him a little about my first year at Cooper Union, in particular about my classes in architectonics and descriptive geometry, both in which I'd excelled, but didn't think he'd be interested. He'd been against my enrolling in the program from the start; he'd thought the focus too narrow for someone so young and had encouraged me to enroll in a liberal arts college instead. For he'd long harbored a distrust of professionals, of experts and specialists of every kind, a disdain for their parochial skills and concerns, for their obedience to money and power, that had turned many a routine trip to the doctor into a grueling object lesson for me.

All I'd known was that I'd wanted nothing to do with my father's world, with his books and journals, his barren politics, his bitter disquisitions on matters so abstruse not even my mother could name them. I'd wanted to escape it all, to do something different with my life. I'd proven good in math and science and had liked to draw, skills for which my father had done nothing to disguise his contempt. The idea of his son becoming an architect was simply inconceivable to him. "And what," he'd pressed me sternly at the dinner table one evening, when I'd first expressed an interest in the work, "what in this hell of all worlds would you build?"

"Why, I wouldn't build anything," I'd replied, thrilled at the chance to correct him but eager not to show it. "I'd only do the drawings, the designs—houses and bridges, perhaps a shopping mall or two."

Luckily my father hadn't pressed me further, only risen from his chair in disgust, for my knowledge of the discipline then was mostly the stuff of fancy, besotted as I'd been by my drawing teacher's own eclectic tastes, by his proclivity for antique prints of the ancient world, woodcuts and lithographs of the architectural wonders of Athens, Carthage, and Damascus, of Cairo, Jerusalem, and Rome.

Among the many artists whose work he'd collected, he'd favored de Neuville, Delsenbach, and Boulée, as well as the incomparable Piranesi, whose baroque and elegiac prints had often snared me in their dreams. For dreams they certainly were, yet so finely observed, so precisely detailed, I'd been tempted to believe, where I'd lounged there on my teacher's couch before his print of the great ruined gallery of the Villa Adriana, that I could step foot inside them, feel the light and shadows on my face, touch the tumbled, overgrown blocks of stone.

It was not that I'd believed, even then, that that was the sort of work that architects did, for I'd seen some actual blueprints before, when we'd added a sunroom to the back of our house. Still it was more to Piranesi that I'd owed my ambition than to any real knowledge of the craft.

My drawing teacher, Mr. Kowalczyk, had lived down the hill from us in a converted old carriage house, which he'd shared with his wife, Zyta, a flashing, erratic woman who, to the best of my memory, never ever stopped moving. Like one of those sharks that must keep swimming to breathe, she was always flitting around us as we worked together in the old tack room he called his studio, sharpening our pencils, opening and closing the windows, and emptying her husband's ashtray after every cigarette he smoked.

In fact, there'd been nothing shark-like about her, for she was tender and witty, she loved American show tunes, and her flesh, when she hugged me, was as spongy as cake.

She'd been a pediatrician in Poland, in Klaisz, where for generations her family had made pianos, and it had been easy for me to picture her there in the cobbled old city I'd conjured in my mind, swabbing sore throats and tapping small knees. I remember thinking she was beautiful, beautiful in the way that my friends' mothers had sometimes seemed beautiful to me when I saw them with their shopping bags in town. Each time she'd ventured into town she'd worn outlandish hats cluttered with flowers, birds' nests, and fruit, chatting easily, gaily, with everyone she met, so that I'd never suspected the way the women in town had mocked her when she passed them in the street. On a number of occasions, I'd spotted her at the old Ithaca Hotel, sitting alone in the large bay window with her teapot and biscuits, looking out at the dreary little street, so lost in her thoughts that she'd never even noticed me.

Yet in her home she was always attentive to me, even gracious, taking my jacket and ushering me into the living room where invariably I'd found waiting for me, on the table between the dark upholstered chairs, a plate of cookies and a glass of ginger ale. I'd especially liked her breasts, which rose plump and powdered from her frilly, low-cut blouses. There was something real and reassuring about them as she leaned over me to examine my drawings, as she often did while I was working, a frank carnality that had brought the blood to my cheeks and made me confident that the earth, for all its tremors, would never stop turning.

I remember late one summer when my mother stopped me on my way down the hill to give me some flowers for Zyta that she'd just cut from our garden. They were roses, I think, for Zyta liked roses best, and I remember sniffing them all the way down the street.

As usual, Mr. Kowalczyk was just finishing up with another student when I arrived for my lesson, a girl from school who'd liked to draw horses, so that I passed straight through the house to where Mrs. Kowalczyk was working in the yard. I enjoyed chatting with her before my lesson and crept up behind her that day, where I found her kneeling in the dirt between the azaleas, holding my breath as long as I could bear it, only to thrust the pretty flowers in her face. Of course she was delighted by the gift and let out a playful shriek but the instant she saw me her face—set to joy—crumpled horribly, her eyes filled with tears, and she bolted inside, dropping her trowel behind her. Her cries brought her husband running but there was nothing I could tell him when he appeared, a fact he grasped in the instant, charging back into the house to find her.

It was only much later that I was able to make any sense of the matter at all. "She once had a son of her own," my mother explained to me over breakfast one morning, some weeks after the school year had begun, sliding a single fried egg onto my toast and looking at me in a way that made the world seem so small I could barely swallow my juice. "In Poland, a boy with freckles like you. Sometimes she gets a little sad."

I was devastated by the news, for I'd often wondered why they'd had no children of their own. I felt powerless, empty, sick, so that even as I rode the bus to school that morning I remember feeling that the world had shrunk, withered round its core, the houses and trees pressing in upon me where I sat alone at the back of the bus until I had to open the window to breathe. And still the sensation persisted, the fear, the feeling, as I tried to picture the boy with freckles like mine, that life, for all its throbbing reality, was but a trick, a ruse.

I'd continued my lessons with Mr. Kowalczyk for another year, though I rarely saw his wife anymore, who spent her days, so he'd once explained to me, 'resting her head' in the bedroom upstairs. Along the staircase, amidst my teacher's favorite illustrations by Pugin and Viollet-le-Duc, he'd hung a number of cheaply framed photographs, mostly of Zyta in her hats, and when alone I'd often examined them, step by step in the dull and shaggy light, as if they might change, as if one day I might discover there in one of them, having somehow missed it before, the precious, shining face of her boy.

As a going-away gift, the day before I left for college, Mr.

Kowalczyk had given me his copy of Piranesi's *Le Carceri*, a handsomely bound collection of the artist's famous prison etchings, and I remember the disappointment I'd felt. Of all of the artist's work, these transcendental dungeons were my least favorite, as they lacked the fine detail, the sheer linear brilliance that distinguished the best of his oeuvre. Dark, irrational, they seemed to have been completed in haste, like sketches for the stage, less renderings than suggestions, hallucinations of grosser, fantastical things. Still it was a beautiful book, an edition I knew he'd treasured for years, and I'd done my best to seem pleased with it, thanking him heartily for all his patience with me and promising to write him as soon as I was settled in New York.

By the time I returned to Ithaca after my first year at Cooper Union, Mr. and Mrs. Kowalczyk had gone. Someone else was living in the old carriage house, a biologist from England named Smith who couldn't tell me anything about their whereabouts. Since taking up residence there he'd received a few letters in their names and had asked me, should I discover a new address for them, if I would see to their redirection. As luck would have it, I never did, though I kept the letters for months before throwing them away.

IBC: 22, 586. HE WAKES with a gasp: Army Cpl. David Aaron Ansky, 22, Bell Gardens, Calif.; died of wounds from an explosive in Samarra; assigned to 4th Battalion, 9th Infantry Regiment, 4th Stryker Brigade Combat Team, 2nd Infantry Division, Fort Lewis, Wash., searches for the clipping in the box by his side when he remembers that his son is not a soldier in Iraq, not from California, not 22, and grins hard to shake the grief that has already stolen through his veins, seizes like a drunk the bright pulsing window, the distant bridge, the wide blue slice of sky, until he remembers it all: the building, the apartment, the room in which he sits, feels the chair rise up beneath him, smells his warm and duplicitous wife, shuddering finally to recognize on the wall beside him the faded old poster from the Brady Museum. And for a moment everything is right again, everything fine. He hears the radio in the kitchen where his wife is listening to the news, smells coffee, lipstick, toast. Upstairs someone (Lily? David?) stumps across the wide plank floors, then the gurgling of pipes in the wall by his chair.

He is eating grapefruit, *The New York Times* draped like a napkin across his knees. The flesh of the fruit is sour-sweet: today is his birthday: at the window the chestnut blooms. He feels giddy, ambitious; the world teeters on his tongue and he thinks of fucking his wife, of surprising her, just now, taking her swan-like at the kitchen sink in a sudden white rush that makes their neighbor, Mrs. Mencken, look up from her tea. But Mrs. Mencken is dead (he huffs to remember, died last spring when the ground was still cold), the kids now bickering upstairs, so that even before he can grip the arms of his chair the moment has passed. And so the day begins: a horse hobbled in the gate.

His daughter Lily has given him a book about trees (here, she points, the chestnut there), David a set of adjustable wrenches, one of which he removes from the stubborn packaging for his son, briefly savoring its balance, its heft, before overturning his chair to test it on one of the bolts beneath the seat. And the boy seems satisfied, if impatiently so, hugging him stiffly, primly, before cracking his way out the door. A car has pulled up at the curb: his girlfriend: Camille.

Camille! The name leaps out like a trout and he is quick to catch it, the slippery fish, to snare it with the gum of other things before the rapids reclaim it: Barrymore, Garbo, Camellia reticulata. He chants, Barrymore, Garbo…, he impetrates, obtests, for he can barely remember the girl (her hands, her face), can barely restrain her fractious French name (garbo, barrymore…), which escapes him now with the color of her voice, her hair, pouring like sand from his fingertips until his hands flop obscenely at the ends of his wrists, a pair of empty sacks. For he is stuffed with sand these days, his preposterous arms and legs, packed to bursting with a thriftless blend of olivine, feldspar, and chert that occasionally trickles from his eyes and ears, and gathers winsomely, each time he pisses, at the bottom of the smooth white bowl. And still he clutches at the name, that golden ring, feels the floor pitch beneath him where he sits, and wonders briefly what death is like, if it is akin to this, but a matter of forgetting, when like a dollop of cream he remembers! Remembers her fat and prinking father (Leloup or Lebeau)—some muckamuck of increments, of math!

Yet it is not enough to stay his fear of slipping, of losing hold, for he cannot reckon the girl herself, as he fears with a shrinking he must, cannot recall what it was she'd done to David that long-ago winter, what it was she'd said to him, withheld, to make him burn down the house each day until he'd hadn't the strength to weep. And then it had passed: the boy had found himself in love again!

Love!

Scratching his stubbled chin, he sees it, the word, through the compound eyes of a fly, sees it like a drop of dirty water on a dirty microscope slide—the greedy, scurrilous life in it, the fumbling, fructuous pluck. Sees with a Leeuwenhoek squint the wriggling, clown-faced sperm. He spies it all in a single putrid drop and longs to reassure his heartsick son, to anoint him with the little he knows about love, to ameliorate with a prayer his darkest, most baleful dreams (Repeat after me: I have seen a good dream, I have seen a good dream, I have seen a good dream!). But the boy is hiding now; lips smeared with chocolate, he is hiding where he always hides, in his mother's long closet, amidst her dresses and shoes. Huddled there in the darkness, he is scarcely there at all, a tender husk of heartbeat and breath upon which so little, so much now depends...

That sound! He sits up, aghast. The television winks: dish soap, green grass, a girl on a trampoline; and suddenly he remembers why his son has come, remembers the maid, not the maid but the heel of her hand in his face. Remembers her shriek, the supple fat about her neck. And he remembers the war (the war!), remembers the murky taste of canned fish and the crackling RAK receiver by his head. Tongue full of light, he bruits the secret plugboard codes (CK IZ QT NP JY GW), tastes breadfruit and taro, sees the blind old Samoan with her teakwood foot who used to beg for cigarettes. For what he remembers now is synoptic, sententious, the mantic muck in the bottom of a cup. And just like that he is happy. His heart leaps up, and in a whisper he croons: Amo, Amas, Amat. Amo, Amas, Amat...

My father is singing again, humming, this time a familiar tune, a Latin conjugation the simple repetition of which once never failed to help me sleep. It is a tune I've often hummed to my daughter, without thinking, as a way of settling her mind at night.

Restless now, I telephone the office in New York to speak with one of my partners, only to be told by his secretary that he is still in a meeting.

I am disappointed that he has not yet responded to my query, a technical question about the ventilation in the numerous wash-down units, my only new e-mail a message from Gina informing me that Rachael's dentist appointment has been changed to next Tuesday, and that she, Gina, will be able to take Rachael to the dentist after all.

Gina has always liked my father and has asked after his health. Once again she has urged me to try to talk to him, to explain what is happening, lest he be overwhelmed by the move.

Of course she is right, though I cannot help but resent the advice, given how callously she treated me. The problem is that I have no idea what to tell him. "It's really a beautiful place," I've thought of saying, pulling up a chair by his side and patting his freckled arm, but have never gotten further than that, repulsed by the idea of pitching the home to him as though it were nothing but a holiday time-share or hotel. For I know the statistics, the facts: the depression, the neglect, the sudden likelihood of premature death.

The last time I mentioned The Villas to him he called me a "shameless little bastard" and warned me that I'd have to drag him from the apartment by his feet, so that more than ever now I miss Gina's confidence with people, her deeply practical sense of life, for she would know exactly what to do now, would know without thinking how to talk to my father, how to lessen what is certain to be a painful adjustment for him. She would tease him, comb his hair, and get him out of his dirty clothes. And she would forbid him to feel sorry for himself, walking him through The Villa's many colorful brochures and insisting that each of the decisions— room size, food plan, number of physical therapy sessions per week—be his.

At first my father had hated Gina: her laughter, her accent, the cut of her hair. He'd deplored her dispassion for life, her ability—the like of which I'd never seen—to resist his political goading. Above all he'd hated her piety, which, he'd insisted, she'd trailed behind her "like a long and noxious veil," though she'd rarely set foot in church. He'd liked to call her my little Virgin Mary.

Yet by the time we'd gotten engaged he'd actually grown quite fond of her, briefly corresponding with her about her work on Tintoretto before turning his back on us for good. For he'd given me an ultimatum one day that if I followed through with my decision to convert to Catholicism he'd consider me dead and gone. And so he had, despite my mother's daily threats and entreaties, so that my mother and sister had attended our wedding without him that May, a beautiful ceremony in St. Teresa's church in the town of Summit, New Jersey where the Ciprianis lived.

It was only after my sister married a black man that my father's feelings for me changed. One day I'd received a phone call from him saying that he would be in New

York for a meeting and would I meet him at Moran's for lunch. I don't remember anything about the lunch itself; all I recall is that my father had misplaced his wallet that day, a fact that had so upset him we'd been forced to leave the restaurant before we'd ordered our food. My guess is that he'd wanted to talk to me about my sister, to make an ally of me, as my mother had resolved to remain neutral in the matter.

The next time I'd seen him was at Thanksgiving that year. Gina was pregnant with Rachael and we'd rented a car to make the trip to Ithaca, picking up Lily and her new husband, Oscar, along the way. We'd met Oscar only once before, at a bar in Chelsea, and, though he'd fallen somewhat short of Lily's description of him, we'd found nothing to dislike in the man. The son of a machinist and a hair dresser in Detroit, he'd dropped out of high school, spent some time in jail, only to earn his G.E.D. and continue on to college in Scranton, Pennsylvania where he was pursuing a degree in electrical engineering.

My father was nowhere to be seen by the time we arrived at the house; my mother had sent him on an errand so that by the time he returned the five of us were comfortably settled in the living room, chatting easily over sandwiches and beer.

I remember he'd stood, rigid, in the doorway, glaring first at Oscar seated awkwardly in the old wingback chair, then at my sister, then at Gina and me, only to settle his eyes upon my mother standing openmouthed at the mantle, whom—so it was clear by his expression—he'd blamed for it all. His face was mottled with anger and for a moment he'd seemed on the verge of speaking, of denouncing us all, when he'd turned on his heels and stormed from the room, when shortly we'd heard his tread on the stairs.

After much pleading my mother had managed to convince him to join us at dinner that evening, for which he hadn't bothered to dress, as was his custom each Thanksgiving, sitting glumly as an overthrown king at the head of the long table in his old khaki pants and chambray shirt and refusing to look at us. The showdown, so long anticipated, appeared to have passed.

But we'd been wrong about that. He'd woken the next day refreshed in his determination to set my sister straight, confronting her the moment he found her alone in the kitchen. Having risen early, I'd just returned from a walk through the neighborhood, surprised by the mass of sensations it had triggered in me, and feeling strangely out of sorts, when I was startled by their shouting.

"Bullshit!" I'd heard my sister scream, just as I closed the front door behind me. "I'll tell you why you hate him. You hate him because he's big and black, because you simply can't bear the thought of a big strong black man fucking your little girl."

Through the kitchen door I'd heard my father chuckle, a cold, disagreeable laugh. "No, my dear," he'd said length. I could picture him shaking his head. "No, I'm afraid it's simpler, even more conventional than that. I don't like him— and this could only come as a surprise to you, Lily—because he's a shifty ex-con who's never held a job in his life."

"But that's not fair! All that happened when he was nineteen, when he was nothing but a kid. He works hard now and you know it."

Again my father had chuckled. "Works hard, does he? So remind me, Lily: how much of the rent is he paying now? Half? A quarter? A tenth? Oh, that's right, he doesn't contribute a cent. You pay it all."

At once I'd heard my sister curse him, something fierce if garbled; I could tell she'd turned her back to him and knew that she was done. Briefly there'd come a clattering of dishes when she'd burst from the kitchen, pushing past me down the hall.

That afternoon I'd driven the two of them to the bus station and for the first time in years my sister had cried to me, sobbing helplessly in my arms. Oscar had gone to get cigarettes and her skinny body had trembled as if trying to shake itself free from the world. Her mascara had left her eyes looking bruised and hollow and I'd nearly told her what I'd felt, what I'd feared in my gut—that she should break it off with Oscar now, before she really got hurt. But I'd bitten my tongue and, when clutching my hands she'd asked me what I thought of him, I'd said I liked him fine.

PULLING UP A CHAIR BESIDE my father now, I cannot think what to tell him, what to say. For it is hard to gauge his awareness, to know how much, at any moment, he is conscious of. He is so still that he could very well be dead but for the shallow heaving of his scarred and hairless chest.

I could tell him that the move is only temporary, a brief hiatus, that he can come back to the apartment as soon as he's recovered and can manage on his own. Or I could tell him the truth, that once he leaves the place tomorrow he will never return. Either way it seems unlikely he'd understand.

To pass the time until Rachael is ready, I've set up a game of chess for us, hoping to engage him, to get a sense of how he feels, but he hardly stirs in his chair. His face is thinner now, his eyes sunken deeply in their sockets, as though all of his vital forces are retreating at once. Even his gums have receded, exposing the cankerous roots beneath them. Amazed, I want to stroke his sweaty head, to comfort him at last, my father, but fiddle with the pieces on the board instead, repulsed suddenly by the spotty, livid pallor of his skin.

Whenever we'd sat for a game of chess when I was a boy, he'd insisted on my being white, on my making the first and often fatal play. For he'd shown me no mercy when we'd faced each other across the kitchen table, no matter my age, his eyes fixed on the board, his fingers twitching in anticipation of his next, decisive move. When it came to chess he'd worshipped the Russians—Chigorin and Levenfish, Smyslov, Botvinnik, and Tal, studying their games with a doggedness that had often left him hollow-eyed and grumpy, come morning, where I'd found him hunched over the board at his desk. He'd liked to memorize their greatest games in order to reenact them for me, pointing out this or that gambit, and providing me with a dynamic appraisal of each and every move. For he'd tried for years to get me involved in the game, buying me my own set, encouraging me to join the chess club at school, and insisting that I sit with him on those rare occasions when a match was broadcast on TV.

Together we'd watched in anguish as Bobby Fischer squandered the first two games in Reykjavik to the Russian Grandmaster, Boris Spassky, before the televised broadcast was terminated, at Fischer's insistence, leaving my father to rehearse the man's blunders again and again on the board in his head in an all but desperate attempt to fathom his tactics. For as much as my father had loved the Russians, he'd soon found himself caught up in the fervor of the times, rooting for the underdog and American, all but possessed by his swift and heretical play. The lengthy match had wreaked havoc on my father's moods, so that only Fischer's victory, after twenty-one games, had been enough to restore his piece of mind.

Not knowing what else to do now, to say, I repeat for my father the little news I know about Lily, hoping to rouse him to some sort of feeling again, to stir the spirits in his scorched and torpid brain.

"You'll never believe it, Dad, but she's back in Ithaca now. She's rented a place on Seneca Street, just a block from our first house," I tell him. "You remember it, just round the corner there—the little red house with the skinny brick walkway. You know, where the Souceks lived. She's rented it out with the option to buy. That is, if all goes well. And I think it will this time. Her boy Simon really likes it there, and Lily's managed to reconnect with a few of her high school friends.

"But it's the job that's really the clincher," I add, uselessly, for he has offered no response at all. "She's working part-time at CAPS, right there on campus, doing assessments and counseling, and she's feeling pretty confident they'll make her a full-time offer soon…

"It's interesting: she says that really nothing in the town has changed, though it's a lot prettier than she remembered it. Of course she's missed the winter this time round. Come December she might be singing a different tune!" I joke, hoping with this to steal a smile from him, but he barely reacts, even when I adjust the pillow behind his head.

The truth is I know very little about Lily anymore. I'd made the mistake last year, when she was still living in Philadelphia, of suggesting that her son Simon might be better off staying with his father for a while. She'd only just recovered from a series of panic attacks that had forced her to stop working and had left her so shaken that Simon had often spent the night at a neighbor's house where, while bathed and fed, he'd been left to himself.

What I hadn't known at the time was that for months she and Oscar had been fighting for custody of the boy, a fight she'd feared she was losing the day I dropped by to see her, so that my timing could not have been worse. The instant the words left my mouth she'd raged at me, as I'd never seen her rage before, punching and kicking me and tearing at my hair, my advice to her—so well-intentioned—just one more betrayal of her affection and trust.

It had all started the year before. She'd been walking back from work one cold winter evening, from the dreary offices where she spent her days counseling pregnant teenaged girls, many of whom were addicts, some dying of AIDS, when she'd encountered one of a half a dozen prostitutes who'd often loitered on the street corner near her building, a familiar young black woman, clearly distinguished beneath her high pink wig and garish makeup by the large, oozing sore on her leg.

Just days before she'd spoken to the woman about the

sore, had encouraged her to get it checked at the free clinic down the street before it turned septic, a simple, professional consideration that had so shaken the young woman that, even before Lily could move to brace her, she'd collapsed against the dirty snow bank, sobbing like a child.

As usual that evening, Lily had recognized the young prostitute where she'd stood stomping her feet to keep warm, and was wondering whether or not to speak to her again, to press her about the sore on her calf, plainly visible through her fishnet stockings, when the woman had spun around and assailed her with a hideous cackling, exposing a mouth of newly broken teeth.

Lily had rushed straight home that evening and curled up in her bed, from which she hadn't emerged until late the next day, after her son had seen himself to school and returned again. And still she'd hardly managed to speak to him at all, to utter a prescient word, barely heard the phone ringing, scarcely noticed when her ex-husband arrived at the apartment, fixed himself a drink, and then drove off with her son.

Sick with remorse now, I take up a copy of the local paper from the stack on the floor by my father's chair and skim the sports section for an article I might read aloud to him while I wait. There is nothing about the Yankees and I settle for an interview with Joe Maddon, the manager of the Tampa Bay Rays, about the upcoming season, a dull, predictable piece that elicits no reaction from my father at all. "How about some local news?" I ask him, feeling foolish, and thumb quickly through the paper, first reading aloud to him a short piece offering tips on beating the upcoming summer heat, then a review of a new Italian restaurant in Bonita Springs, and finally an article about a 64 year-old man who'd recently defended himself from robbers by attacking them with a meat cleaver he kept by his bed. Discouraged, I look for something else to read to him but the only alternative at hand is the prayer book in his lap.

In fact it is not a siddur but an interlinear translation of a book called the Pirkei Avot, a short collection of rabbinical maxims I've seen before, and briefly I scan the pages between which he has tucked the ribbon to mark his place, selecting a passage at random and intoning the ancient words with a solemnity I do not feel: "Rabbi Chanina son of Tradyon would say: Two who sit and no words of Torah pass between them, this is a session of scorners, as is stated, "And in a session of scorners he did not sit (Psalms 1:1)." A session of scorners. Is that what we are, a session of scorners?

Outside the breeze has picked up a little, rustling the dry palm fronds below, and groggy as I am I try to think of all I've left to do before Wednesday, when Rachael and I are scheduled to fly back to New York, from where, the very next day, I'll be off again to El Paso. For the work in New Mexico is progressing more quickly than I'd expected; the footings are in, the foundation complete, so that for the first time I should be able to see the outline of the complex from the air.

Since first settling on the design for the project last year, I've often imagined some passenger aboard a 727 en route to San Diego or L.A. waking from a nap and peering reflexively out the scratched plastic window by his seat, only to glimpse—like a vision from a nightmare, a dream—my sprawling labyrinth in the desert below. It is the way I first saw the ruins of Borobudur, through a break in the clouds from the window of a Cessna 350, which some Javanese clients had hired in order to show me the eastern part of the island. "A diagram of the universe!" one of them had scoffed aloud to me, pressing his sallow face to the window and derisively sucking his teeth.

I'd rarely dreamt of my work, though the jobs have been as varied as their settings unique, sealing off the plans and problems each night in a special place in my brain where they could only be tapped again come daylight, after a hot shower and a pot of strong coffee. Then one night, just after the deal on this latest project in New Mexico was closed, I'd dreamt of Gunadharma, the legendary architect of Borobudur, of how he'd had to dream the great stupa a thousand nights running before he'd permitted its construction to begin. I'd seen the hillside cleared, the earth roughly terraced, heard the musical clink-clinking of a thousand chisels on stone.

It was a vision that recurred to me, night after night, for weeks in succession, and with little variation, so that even when I'd paced the desert in my dreams, following the lines of my labyrinth in the sand, Gunadharma had hovered just above my head, speaking cryptically, pedantically, of the ancient laws of vāstuśāstra—of devas and naksatras, of dai-vikapāda, mānusapāda, and paiśācapāda, the sacred quarters of gods, men, and ghosts. And in my dreams I'd seen my temple rising, block by block, slab by slab, until I could pace its corridors alone, thrilled, appalled at heart, by the spiral-ing echo of my steps.

Now suddenly the dreams have ceased; the vision is gone.

THE NIGHT BEFORE LAST, THE night before we were due to fly down here, I'd been unable to sleep, pacing the floor of my apartment in anxious expectation of the trip. For I'd expected the worst, had anticipated finding my father dead in his chair or lying naked in a pool of urine on the bathroom floor.

I'd tried for days to reach him, eager only to hear his voice, strategically timing my calls in the hope of catching him off-guard, of startling a reaction from him, but he'd refused to answer the phone, just as my mother had feared. With no other recourse, short of calling for an ambulance, I'd telephoned his neighbor, Mrs. Katz, a dark, agoraphobic woman who rarely ventured out of doors but in the early morning hours, when she carried her trash down the hall.

At first she'd refused to help me, claiming this and that ailment, that she was crippled by migraines, by arthritis, by gout, when at last—for no reason I could fathom—she'd agreed to do it, promising that evening to check on him, to see that he was fine. Yet she too had failed to get a response from him, rapping loudly on his door with her cane before scurrying back to her apartment, though not before determining that he was indeed still alive, if rudely, irascibly so. For wasn't that what I'd wanted to know?

She'd heard him through the door, she'd attested plainly to me, if with a hint of indignation, had discerned what she was certain was the switching of television channels inside, and later, through the wall that divided their apartments, the familiar roar of his toilet, a shuddering of pipes that shook the teacups on her dining room shelf.

Of course I'd been relieved by the news, though even now, knowing that my father is safe, I've been unable to sleep, let alone to dream, too troubled by the matters at hand to consider my life, my work.

Perched at the kitchen counter last night, long after I'd seen my father and Rachael to bed, I'd studied the plans of the project on my laptop, poring over the details in the hope of quickening the lambent vision until I'd collapsed around 2 a.m., only to be torn from my stupor by the sound of my father weeping.

It had been enough to keep me awake for the remainder of the night, so that now it is everything I can do not to curl up on the sofa and sleep. For there is still so much to do. I need to finish clearing out my father's study, to sort through the boxes in storage downstairs, and to arrange for the carpets to be cleaned. And I must remember to give the real estate agent a call, as she is eager see the apartment sold, a prospect that fills me with regret. For it is hard to imagine another couple here, calling to one another through the rooms, eating their meals in the little kitchen, and enjoying the sunset each evening from their chairs on the lanai.

It was my mother who had found the apartment in the sheltered little enclave of Punta Rassa, she who'd fallen in love with the light, the view. She'd had the place redecorated at once, painting the walls, tearing up the carpets, and replacing the living room furniture they'd brought with them from Ithaca with a brightly-upholstered rattan suite that had offended my father as much for its style as for its price. She'd wanted nothing to do with their former life, putting all of their artwork, their Stenbergs, Shahns, and Lissitskys, their grim German etchings, into storage in the basement and hanging the work of local artists instead. She hadn't cared if it was good or not—a seashell, two cows in a field—only that it was fresh and simple and took nothing from the light.

She'd changed her appearance as well; within their first few weeks in Florida she'd cut and colored her hair, joined an aerobics class, and given away her old sweaters and dresses, spurred by a Punjabi friend of hers to wear nothing again but loosely fitting cottons and silks. And it was she who had chosen the west coast of Florida as the place where they would live, disappointing my father and many of their friends from New York, who'd retired some years before them to the more popular Atlantic coast, to the heavily Jewish communities of Boca Raton, Ft. Lauderdale, and West Palm Beach. I remember she'd been adamant about the choice, refusing, this time, "to settle for the same damned thing."

A session of scorners. Tracing the embossed lettering on the soft leather cover, I flip through a few more pages of the slender volume, saddened and amazed to think that all of my father's efforts, all of his striving and struggle, have boiled down to this, the atavism of a housecat still roused by the flutter of birds.

For as long as I can remember my father's Jewishness has never been anything more than an accident of fate, a fact as random and meaningless as the color of his hair or the size of his feet. Except of course when it came to Hitler. And even then his response, for all its vehemence, had always seemed to me more simply human than Jewish, his passions stirred more by a general sense of outrage than by some aching tribal wound. Yet it's clear I've been wrong about this, wrong all along, that, at least as regards my father, I've underestimated the grip of such things. Watching him pray this morning, it was as if the Prophets themselves had reached forward to claim him.

At breakfast this morning I'd asked Rachael if she'd like to select some of my mother's shells to keep as mementos for herself, but she'd promptly declined the offer, looking up from her book only long enough to tell me that she'd never really had an interest in shells.

I'd wanted to reproach her, to rebuke her for her lack of feeling, as I'd simply been unwilling to believe that she'd mistaken my meaning, my tone. Yet as I'd watched her turning the pages of her book between bites of cereal, clearly oblivious to my presence at the table beside her, to the fact that she'd hurt me, to the autistic-like bobbing of her once-proud grandfather in his filthy white chair, I'd realized in a flash that I myself was to blame. For she'd never been sentimental about family, about my family, that is, never very curious about me. When in her first year at St. Clare's she'd been asked to make a family tree, she—a student who'd excelled at everything—had actually balked at the task, completing the project only under duress and then refusing to present it in class.

It is a feeling, an ambivalence, for which I can hardly fault her, as over the years I've told her little about my childhood, my past. Without intending to (or has it always been my intention?) I've begrudged her even the simplest details about my youth, about my childhood in Ithaca, about Lily and my parents, whose lives—so fraught and conflicted—are such an integral part of my own. Once finished with high school, I'd been so impatient to get away, so eager to break with those years, that I'd never considered the possibility of a juncture like this, a day when I'd want to recoup it all, to remember, explain. For how else is Rachael to forgive me, to embrace me, but within the context of my own particular past?

Yet how to begin? That over the years she's been drawn more to her mother's side of the family is hardly surprising. All her life she's been immersed in the love and humor of Gina's large family, her mother's childhood tales corroborated a thousand times by her grandparents, Chiara and Adalberto, and by her gregarious aunts and uncles—so numerous, so akin in cast and character, that I've never managed to keep them straight.

What, given this, would she want with my mother's dusty shells? Why, she must scarcely remember my mother at all, except perhaps as the smiling, silver-haired woman in the photograph on my desk. And my father? How, given his condition, given how little she knows of him, could she feel anything but revulsion for the caustic old man? It is a thought that saddens me, for if my father seems a stranger to me, his son, to my daughter he must seem nothing but a ghost, some churlish ancestral spirit to be placated, twice daily, with a generous serving of platitudes and pills. Yet there is more to the man than this, if only she could see it.

Suddenly my father mutters beside me, licking his cracked, dry lips. I find him staring at me, amazed, as if only now has he realized I'm here. Then, just as suddenly, he scowls, his dark, overgrown eyebrows twitching like bugs.

"She took it again!" he snarls. "Didn't I tell you she would?"

"Took what, Dad? And who?"

"The remote, what else?" he snaps, searching frantically about him in his chair. "She's been sneaking around me all morning trying to get her grubby little hands on it."

"Are you talking about the maid?" Yesterday he told me that the maid had been pilfering his things—his bourbon, his glasses, the newspaper clippings he keeps in a box by his chair.

"Yes, the maid. That little Mexican. I thought I told you to get rid of her."

"Dad, there hasn't been a maid here in weeks. Remember? You struck the last one with your cane."

"Yeah? Then who the hell is that?" he sneers triumphantly, stabbing a crooked finger at Rachael who has just appeared in the doorway beside me. "You there: I thought I told you to leave me alone!"

"Dad, she's not the maid. She's your granddaughter, Rachael. Come here, sweetie," I whisper, taking her by the hand so that my father can see her better.

"Granddaughter, hell. Why, she's brown as a nut! Now listen, you, whatever your name is, I want my damned remote."

"Look, Dad, the remote's right here. I just replaced the batteries for you."

"No, no. I'm talking about the other one," he barks impatiently. "The one you brought me from New York."

"This is the one I brought you from New York. See? The old one's over there," I explain, as calmly as I can, but he ignores me, his eyes fixed on Rachael who stands stiffly beside me.

"You know, she took your mother's shoes," he declares, sneering at Rachael, whose face has darkened with humiliation, and I'm about to send her away, to ask her to wait downstairs for me, when she snorts with derision, shaking her head at him.

"See there. See the way she looks at me? The little bitch. Just ask her yourself. That's right. I had them bound up in a box to give to Mrs. Katz when all of a sudden they disappeared. Gone. Vanished. Or so I thought. But, no! The very next day little miss you-know-who here shows up for work with her feather duster and mop and what do you think she's got on her feet? I mean, the gall of it!" he hisses at her. "Right under my nose!"

"Dad, this is Gina's girl. You remember Gina."

"Gina?" he repeats, cocking his head, and for a moment the name seems to tug at him when his face goes blank, the anger, the indignation, gone. The name has clearly thrown him, his eyes glassy, his lips fluttering as if to speak, when he recognizes the remote control in his hand and switches on the set, filling the room with its noisome chatter.

I wait until Rachael is gone before saying goodbye. "Dad. Dad, we're going now. To check out your new room at The Villas, remember? Is there anything you need?" I add, out of habit, for he rarely replies. Reluctant to leave him, I squeeze his bony shoulder, but he only grins at the brightly pulsing screen.

I FIND RACHAEL DOWNSTAIRS BY the car, a nondescript

Chrysler we rented at the airport. Arms folded across her chest she refuses to look at me. The humidity has made her hair curlier than she likes it, a look, like the way she clutches her handbag, I find becoming for the way it reminds me of her mother.

"I'm sorry about that," I say, searching for the right words to comfort her, though it is more for my father that I feel sorry. "He doesn't mean what he says."

"I don't care what he means. I just want to go home."

"And we will. Soon," I tell her, stroking her cheek, when I get an idea. "Listen, why don't we take Nana's Mercedes instead? I can put the top down and later we can go for a drive along the beach."

I still have the keys to my mother's convertible where she left it parked in the garage. I'd surprised her with it, the year before she died, had had it delivered to her as a Mother's Day gift, a bright red ribbon affixed to the hood. True to form, my father had insisted she refuse it (a reckless, vulgar gift, with money got from God knows where), but she'd simply ignored him, as had been her habit by then, stroking the fine upholstery and gently shaking her head. Just last week I'd managed to sell it to a woman in New York, a widow who lives half the year in Punta Rassa. All that remains is to send her the keys.

The moment I start the engine Rachael fiddles with the radio until she finds a station she likes and soon we are on our way.

THREE

THE DRIVE TO The Villas takes us up to McGregor then over the Caloosahatchee to Cape Coral. Feet tapping the dashboard, Rachael is quiet for most of the way, occasionally humming along with the jangly tunes. Only when we reach the turn-off for The Villas does she sit up in her seat as if charged with a sudden apprehension, though her face—so smooth, unblemished—reveals little to me.

The entrance, framed by a pair of ghoulish-looking banyan trees, gives way to a winding drive lined with royal palms that inspires the impression that one is approaching a fancy club or hotel, though the complex itself, appearing suddenly from behind a grassy knoll, is remarkably modest in its pretensions, its cream-colored buildings largely functional and unadorned, their only embellishment the flowering hibiscus beneath the windows and the large old jacaranda in the circle out front.

We are met at the door by a pleasant young woman in a white blouse, tight skirt, and quick-clicking heels who guides us past the empty lounge to the elevator by the front desk, which together we take to the second floor where I've chosen a corner room for my father. Rachael goes at once to the window, pushing aside the heavy drapes and looking down upon the graveled yard as if it were the only way to assess the place, by its relation to the world outside.

Not knowing that I've seen the room before, our solicitous young guide seizes the opportunity to enumerate its many features for me, which she checks off, as from a list in her head—the private bathroom, the personal telephone, the flat-screen satellite TV. And she is pleased to tell me, briefly plopping herself down on the corner of the bed before snapping to her feet again, that the twin-sized mattress (designed by a leading orthopedist) is new.

"As you can see, Mr. Ansky, we've taken the liberty of decorating the place," she explains, indicating, with a theatrical sweep of her hand, the rocking chair and rag rug in the corner, the nebulous seascape over the bed, and, by the door, the tawdry assortment of knickknacks on the tall chest of drawers. "Needless to say, your father—It is your father, right?—is free to decorate the place as he sees fit. The important thing is that he feel comfortable here, that he feel himself at home," she assures us, when, with a thrust of her pointy chin, she indicates the two small cases at my feet. "I see you've brought a few of his things."

"Yes, just some odds and ends I'd like to set out for him before he arrives tomorrow."

"Well then I'll leave you to it," she replies with a crisp if courteous smile, opening the door to go. "If you have any questions you'll find me at the desk downstairs."

She has just left us when the door opens again and in pops her wavy blonde head. "By the way, there's a hammer and nails in the drawer there by the bed. In this plaster I find the little nails work best."

I give Rachael the job of arranging my father's things: his time and tide clock; a nautical chart of Lake Cayuga; the faded gray watercolor of his Fletcher-class destroyer, the USS Chevalier, which he'd painted in '43 while serving aboard ship as a radio operator; as well as a half a dozen framed photographs of my mother and Lily and me.

In the meantime I distribute his clothes (his underwear, khaki pants, pajamas, and socks) in the three large dresser drawers, which have been freshly papered and scented with cedar. In the closet, large enough for four men his age, I hang a new striped bathrobe, a single white dress shirt, his navy blazer, and the pale green windbreaker he used to keep on his boat. Finally, on the floor of his closet, I line up his slippers and shoes.

The room I've chosen for my father is called a Junior Suite, though it is only a single room with a bathroom and a nook like the heel of shoe. In the nook they've placed an overstuffed chair that appears to have been miniaturized, through some miraculous process, to fit the space exactly. Beside it, on a spindle-legged table, stands a darkly shaded lamp. While clearly the nook was designed as a place for reading and reflection, it is hard to imagine my father ever sitting there, let alone reading a book, and I'm struck again by how much, how expressly, the look and feel of the place—the rooms, the amenities, the grounds—have been designed with the residents' families in mind.

As a part of the furnishings, a little table with chairs has been set before the window, as for a tête-à-tête between friends. It is there upon the table that I place my father's chess set, taking the time to arrange the pieces on the handsome old board.

Rachael has chosen a spot on the wall by the window to hang my father's clock, which I attend to with the hammer and nails from the drawer, stepping back from the wall, once I'm finished, to assess the job with her. She likes it fine, she says and moves to the bed to consider the photos I've set out for her on the pale blue counterpane, looking up now and then to decide where to place them.

One of the photographs, one of Lily and me in the back-yard of our house in Ithaca, was taken by my mother shortly after we'd purchased the ramshackle inn. There behind us I can make out the corner of the old potting shed, which we'd had demolished soon after our arrival. Infested with termites, it had been used for storing the bicycles the widow had provided as a service to her guests. I remember the bikes themselves, rusty, thick-framed Huffmans with metal bas-kets, braced fenders, and white walled tires, which we'd sold as a lot to a junkman in town.

I recall feeling, in our initial weeks in Ithaca, that every-thing was new, that anything could happen, that I might wake in my new bedroom one morning to find the entire world had changed. I kept looking for signs, tracking my mother and father through their days like a bloodhound sniffing for clues. When my father laughed, when he washed the dishes for my mother, when he carried my sister to bed, I was certain that the change had come at last, holding my breath and closing my eyes to be certain not to jinx it. More than anything I'd hoped that we'd be happy there, in Ithaca, that my father, after all his struggles, would succeed.

I'd loved the house then, before we'd refurbished it and made it our own—the crystal doorknobs, ratty carpets, moldy samplers, and dark organza drapes. I'd been fascinated by the transom windows throughout, opening and closing them with a metal rod designed for the purpose and working with my father, on the one above the kitchen door, to strip the thick white paint from the glass.

We'd found the rooms much as the widow had left them, the rotting chintz and peeling plaster, the black iron bedsteads with their hand-stitched quilts, the books and magazines in the parlor downstairs, the pages curled and yellowed with age. Even the dining room cupboard, with its cups and saucers, its soup bowls and plates, had remained untroubled by human hands. Mr. Rabinovich had seen to that. Only the kitchen had been cleared out, the drawers and cabinets stripped bare, the door of the old Coldspot left conspicuously ajar.

I'd never considered the place haunted, though for weeks at the start my sister had complained of lost possessions, of strange knockings in the wall by her bed. The house had simply felt full to me, as if the air inside had yet to release that dense human moisture it had absorbed in its many years as a small hotel.

I'd liked to picture the guests (a few of whose names I knew from the ledger we'd found in the widow's desk) taking their breakfast in the darkly-papered parlor, sipping their tea and coffee and exchanging the sort of pleasantries I'd read about in books. There'd been a pair of sisters named Jarvie and a salesman 'D. Winkler' from Poughkeepsie whom I'd always pictured in a Tattersall vest, a stout, gregarious man with a red nose and sandy-colored mustache who'd liked to make the ladies blush with his stories of the nightlife in Paris just after the war. He'd often stayed in my room, the room that was to become my own, the simple brass number of which I'd asked my father to leave on the door, for I'd liked very much the feeling, each time I'd entered my room, that I myself was a guest there in a pension or hostel in some strange, dark city halfway round the world.

I'd often imagined his routine, this Mr. D. Winkler, after a long day of peddling his wares in the towns around the lake: the methodical undressing, the glass of whiskey by the bed, the abstracted massaging of his small and wrinkled feet. I'd had only to whisper his name to know the loneliness he'd felt each night as he'd readied himself for bed. For certainly he was a lonely man, spending weeks on the road before returning home to a room that was also like my room, where he'd poured himself a whiskey, then, tug by tug, unlaced his leather shoes.

For weeks, after we'd first moved in, I'd studied the widow's things, as I'd found them ranged about the house, eager to know more about the kindly old woman who'd wandered out to the gorge, one bitter cold night, in nothing but a housecoat and boots. For I couldn't help believing that such anguish as she'd suffered there had left its fragile traces, settling like pollen, like dust, in dark and unswept nooks. Her own small room had been of particular interest to me. To better accommodate her guests, she'd made a bedroom for herself in the sewing room at the head of the stairs, with its curious collection of ratty silks and satins and Chinoiserie, the only natural light in which fell red upon her desk through a pane of scarlet glass. There, amidst her wigs and liniments, I'd found her girdles and dresses boxed like hats beneath her bed.

It was by all accounting a dreary old house that defied my mother's attempts to brighten its lugubrious mood, though she'd hung new curtains, painted the walls, and filled the rooms with flowers. My sister had liked to call it "The Tower," after the story of Rapunzel made famous by the Brothers Grimm. For she'd never tired of describing the way our father had trapped our mother there, in Ithaca, cutting her off from her friends and surroundings, so as to control her completely. She believed he'd felt so threatened by our mother's intelligence, by her promise as a scholar, that it had been the only way to prevent her from surpassing him.

Yet it was our mother's beauty he'd feared most; such was my sister's contention. Our mother had been a graduate student of his at Columbia, her beauty so keen, so uncanny, that he'd had to move quickly to seduce her, meeting with her over coffee to talk about her work and treating her to the occasional dinner and show. But not even their engagement and wedding had been enough to assuage my father's fears of losing her. Sixteen years her senior, and wildly jealous of her time and attention, he'd not been happy until he'd locked her away in the dark old house on the hill where, finally, without rivals, he could call her his own.

Yet in the end his plan had backfired, so Lily had insisted to me, some many years later, after the table was cleared and Gina and Rachael had gone to bed. For it was he himself who had led the handsome Michael Radetsky to our door. Our father had gotten exactly what he deserved, she'd gloated bitterly, pleased to think he'd suffered so deeply, that fate had dealt him such a wholesome blow. Yet by the time we'd finished the dishes her anger at him had dissipated.

Made maudlin by the wine, she'd repeated for me the story of how, for her eleventh birthday, he'd taken her to The Ritz for tea, only to end our evening together by calling him on the phone.

Still I'd recognized the truth in what she'd said, the fact that he'd felt threatened by his young wife's intelligence and beauty, and by her many friendships there in New York, so many of them with men. Surely he'd hated the way his colleagues had circled round her at a party, touching her naked arms and back and whispering secrets in her ears, secrets she'd dismissed as trifles and refused to discuss with him when he'd pressed her about them on their taxi rides home. All of it was true. Yet there was more to his flight than that.

When offered the job at Cornell, he'd jumped at the chance to escape New York, not only because he'd wanted to possess my mother more fully, nor simply because he was tired of the hustle and bustle, as he'd claimed. He'd also wanted to leave New York because he'd suddenly realized, somewhere deep inside himself, that he could no longer compete with his Columbia colleagues, most of whom were publishing regularly, a few of them already celebrities in the field.

His book on Trotsky was to have saved him, distinguished him at last, though it seems clear to me that even then, as we were packing our bags for Ithaca, he'd known that the book would not redeem him, that the study—whatever its merits— would never prove enough. In any case, New York had been his father's city, the city where Joseph Ansky had made his name. Surely my father had suffered the fact for years, had realized at last that if ever he was to get out from under his father's long shadow he'd have to strike out on his own.

BESIDE ME ON THE BED, Rachael is gazing at a photograph of my young mother standing at a railing by the sea. There is something about it that puzzles her, and just as I'm about to speak, she says, "She was beautiful, wasn't she?"

Rachael has rarely ever spoken of my mother and I feel a sudden surge of affection for her, a warmth, a gratitude, I hesitate to express for fear it will silence her once more. "Yes," is all I say.

"How old do you think she was here?"

Briefly I take the photo from her to consider it more closely. It's been a while since I've seen it. "Hard to know, really, but she must be thirty-five, thirty-six."

"Hmm," replies Rachael, skeptically, taking back the photo. "I think she looks younger than that. Twenty-seven, twenty-eight. I think she looks a lot like Lily."

"Really?" I reply, peering over her shoulder.

"Yes, but happier. She looks happy there."

"Yes, she does, doesn't she? She usually was," I add, by the way, for mostly I remember her smiling. "People often said that about her, that she seemed happy."

"Do you know where it was taken?" asks Rachael.

"No. I'm afraid I don't. But here, let me see it," I say. "If I open up the frame maybe we'll find a clue."

Sure enough the photo is labeled: I recognize my mother's handwriting at once—Barcelona '68—and the flood of memories is so sudden, so intense, that for a moment I am speechless. For I was there when the photo was taken; I must have been. Who knows, I myself might have taken the picture, though by the look in my mother's eyes—at once self-conscious and coy—it suddenly seems unlikely, as I sense another presence there, a finer, more discriminate eye.

Upon the invitation of one of my mother's friends from college, a woman named Carina Figueras, she and I had taken a trip to Barcelona that year. Just the two of us. Not only had my mother been eager to see her old friend, who'd promptly returned to Spain after completing her degree in New York, but she'd long had a dream of visiting Barcelona itself, of strolling La Rambla and of seeing with her own two eyes Antoni Gaudí's incomparable creation, La Sagrada Família.

I remember now how at first she'd bickered with my father who'd flatly rejected her suggestion that the four of us make the trip together. For he'd been adamant about the matter, refusing to even consider a visit to Spain until 'the rank old bastard' Franco was dead. When, in frustration, my mother had threatened to go alone, he'd berated her fiercely, drinking too much gin and sulking in his study for days, only to rouse her from sleep one night to bless her plan, a plan that, somehow, in the end, had included me.

I have only the vaguest memories of the trip—watching a detective movie on the airplane, huddled snugly beside my mother; the angry buzz of mopeds in the streets; the sun-struck view of tiled rooftops from the bathroom window of her friend Carina's apartment on the edge of Barri Xinès. Most of what I remember about the trip I remember second-hand, through my mother's subsequent descriptions of it.

For her it had been a dream come true; indifferent to my father's prejudices, she'd wanted only to wander the narrow streets of the city and to sit in the park before La Sagrada

Família, gazing up at its soaring, apostolic towers. Never religious, she'd been drawn there by the sheer madness of Gaudí's dream; by its yearning, Babel-like audacity; by its haunting, irrefragable presence in stone.

True to his word, my father had not set foot on Spanish soil until Franco was dead, booking a flight to Madrid, some many months later, where he'd taken a room at the Villa Real, slept a dreamless night, then hired a taxi to Santa Cruz del Valle de los Caídos where he'd spat on the fascist's grave.

Rachael, distracted by the photo of my mother, has lowered her guard, so that suddenly she looks the little girl again, her skinny legs crossed beneath her on the bed, her expression simple, uncontrived, and it is everything I can do not to stroke her cheek. For she is more beautiful in this moment than I have seen her in years, more beautiful than I can fathom with these tired old eyes, which fill so quickly between blinks that the effort is blinding. I want to tell her everything, want at last to avouch myself in full before she frowns at me and sighs. Instead I risk it all: "You may have it, if you like."

"The picture?" she says, surprised.

"Yes, if you like," I reply, picking quickly through the other framed photos on the bed in order to seem distracted, though the tension I feel is so great I have to rise from the bed. The seconds swell, the pressure builds in my head and chest, when, impatient with her silence, and desperate to cut myself free, I reach for the only thing I can think of to say. "Do you think he'll be alright?"

"Grandpa?"

"Yes."

Impassive, she looks around the room, at the walls, the ceiling, the floor. "I think he'll be lonely," she says.

"But he's lonely now. He must be," I protest, at which remark she only shakes her head.

"He'll be very lonely here. He's not so lonely now."

Of course, it is something she couldn't possibly know, though I let it pass, parting the curtains to consider the yard below. She couldn't possibly know what the old man is feeling, couldn't possibly fathom the workings of his dry and twisted heart.

We arrange the last of my father's things in silence and soon we are ready to go. For some reason I'd felt compelled to bring my father's old typewriter, which I set its case by the chair in the nook. If nothing else he might remember it, might recall the touch of the keys, might tap out a letter, a note. Who can say?

Rachael is pleased with our work. She takes one more tour about the room before smoothing out the counterpane where she'd been sitting, then folds back the top of it, plumping the fresh white pillows in preparation for my father's head. The photo of my mother has vanished.

SOME DAYS HE DREAMS OF the Winter Palace on the bitter lemon Neva, stalks its lavish halls, mounts and descends its 117 staircases. Some days he jiggles the knobs and peers behind each of its 1,886 doors, looks at once at the wavy stars and river through its 1,945 crown glass eyes. He prefers to think of the palace empty, hollow as an Easter egg, hollow as a skull, prefers to pace the enfilade alone, counting his steps, his breaths, making a catalogue of death camps, of ships. He likes to think of the palace in snow, the great square empty, the chthonic black river arthritic with cold. For he remembers the winter best, the shrunken days and drunken nights; he remembers crossing the bridge to Vasilievsky Island one particularly gelid night and gazing back across the Neva to see the palace ablaze against the darkness like a liner lost at sea.

He remembers this; then the ghosts rise up. He remembers their names, the men and women, Stalin's faithful Jewish dead: Lozovsky, Yuzefovich, Zuskin, Fefer, Talmy, Markish, Teumin, Hofshteyn, Bergelson, Shimeliovich, Kvitko, Zheleznova, Vatenberg, Vatenberg-Ostrovskaya, Bregman, and Shtern. He remembers their testimonies, the photographs, the bruise on Khayke's cheek. And he remembers the strange despondency he'd felt as a student there amidst such gilded ruins, remembers with pity, with shame, his father's many letters to him—sometimes two and three a week—with their effete and degenerate cant. He'd written his father only once, a reply so terse, so niggard of fact and feeling, he remembers its wording to this day: Dear Dad, Just back from a walk along Nevsky Prospekt. More cold today. Feeling fine.

The trip back from The Villas is fast. As promised, I drive Rachael south along the beach, Ft. Myers Beach, stopping before a row of t-shirt shops near the pier so that we can walk on the sand, which we do, leaving our shoes in the car.

The afternoon sun is surprisingly hot; out in the bay a pair of sailboats tacks its way north against the breeze. It had been just such a day when my father and I consigned my mother's ashes to the sea. He'd hired a man he knew at the marina to take us out in his boat that afternoon, a sleek Tartan Cruiser in the teakwood cabin of which my father had sat alone with the packet of ashes until we'd reached Cabbage Key. Only then had he appeared on deck, squinting at the bright light and swaying unsteadily on his loosely sandaled feet. He'd suddenly looked different to me, my father, as if in his short time in the cabin alone, he'd shed a hundred leathery selves, so that all that remained to contain him, when at last he'd emerged from below, was a pouch of pink and tender skin.

He'd had no blessings to say, as might have been recited a hundred years ago, only held the paper packet before him in his hands, held it out above the sparkling water like a sailor of old his offering to some vengeful goddess of the deep. And he hadn't shed a tear that day, though once the packet was gone, once it had vanished beneath the waves, he'd sat crumpled in the stern, indifferent as death itself to the sea and sky, flinching not a muscle when the wind plucked the hat from his head.

At the sight of the pier Rachael skips ahead of me, only to stop suddenly to consider a pair of sandpipers foraging in the surf beside her. She has never struck me as a contemplative child, the sort to pause and wonder, though I know so little about her anymore that all such judgments seem moot. I watch her as she studies the restive birds, when I remember something my mother once told me. Not long after she and my father were settled here in Florida, when we were out searching for shells one morning, she'd told me that when she died she hoped to return here as a sandpiper, to return to this very beach. Nearly forgotten, the memory makes me smile, and for a moment I study the pipers ahead of us as they chase the lacy skirt of surf, grateful for this simple souvenir.

Now Rachael signals to me; she has reached the pier and I wave her on, intending to join her there, beneath the shelter at the end, where a half a dozen fishermen stand idly with their crab lines and rods. At once she is mine again, the little girl I knew and loved, and a stranger to me, too, some other man's child. For I hardly know what to make of her now. We have grown so far apart in recent years that I fear I'll never be able to make up the ground with her before she's off to college and out on her own. By now there is so much unspoken between us that we have little left to say. And I blame her mother for this, for not teaching her to speak to me, to care what I say.

The last time I met with Gina we'd argued about Rachael's confirmation ceremony, now less than a month away. We'd argued churlishly about the date and about the ceremony itself—about the guests and responsibilities and reception to follow. For I'd been angry with her for the way I'd been excluded from the planning. Indeed she hadn't bothered to consult me at all.

Upon the death of Rachael's godmother, a woman named Margaret Fay, Gina had chosen her youngest brother, Tony, to replace the old woman, a decision with which she'd known I would never have agreed, having never liked the shiftless man, the black sheep of the family, who'd recently spent a term in jail for malware fraud.

The truth is, neither the guests nor the responsibilities nor even her miscreant brother Tony was to blame for my anger at her. I'd realized only later that I was angry at Gina for something else: I was angry at her for the fact that, though indeed I'd converted to Catholicism to marry her (for such would have been her simple rebuttal of me), she'd refused to discuss how we were to raise our child, to flesh out, if such fleshing out had still been possible then, the sort of future we'd envisioned for Rachael, the sort of person we'd hoped she'd become.

Now that our marriage has been annulled, now that it never was, it seems too late to consider such things, as if the die has been cast and there is nothing I can do. Within a few weeks Rachael will receive the Holy Spirit and in this way affirm her commitment to the Church. And while I'm not troubled by her Catholicism per se, which I suspect she'll wear lightly in the years to come, if she wears it at all, I fear she'll never care that she is also Jewish, that through me, her father, she is sprung from different, darker roots, roots that if nourished might produce their own strange beauty, too.

For this I can hardly blame Gina, as she never asked me to choose. Happy, magnanimous, I'd taken it upon myself to convert to Catholicism as a measure of my affection for her, as a gesture of good will to her family and friends. Having never felt particularly Jewish, it had seemed a simple thing to do. It was only after my father had collapsed in grief at the news of it that I'd fully grasped the nature of my decision; the scales had fallen from my eyes, my every step a hollow step, my every prayer a hollow prayer, so that when at last the day arrived and I'd stood before the priest in his church I'd stood there nakedly, then and forever a Jew, his faith but a deadness in my chest.

By the time I join Rachael at the end of the pier she has struck up a conversation with one of the fisherman, an older man in filthy shorts and t-shirt, who is telling her about his multi-hook rig, specifically designed, he claims, for fishing from piers. To my surprise she seems genuinely interested in what he says, fingering the hooks and examining his simple rod, which—much to my wonder—he permits her to hold.

So as not to disturb them, I take a seat on the weathered bench before the small tackle shop there, shielding my face from the sun. Flies, attracted by the litter of fish scales and bait, are gathered so thickly in spots that from a distance they look like holes in the planks. Tired, I close my eyes for a moment, lulled by the sound of the waves beneath me and by the quarrelsome chatter of gulls overhead. Shadows flicker across my eyelids; I see specks of dust—wormlike, bacilliform, when with a sudden prickling of my skin I realize I'm being watched. There, on the just roof above me, sits a large gray pelican eying me with a critical intensity that reminds of my father, of the way he used to watch me at the table as I chewed. The pelican blinks, clacks its bill at me, then flexes its mighty wings before lumbering off through the thick and sultry air.

The fisherman has allowed Rachael to drop a line into the water below, her excitement evident in her voice and in her lightly dancing feet. Something in the moment reminds me of Israel, of the summer we spent as a family in Tel Aviv.

I'd won my firm a job there, a project to design a large detention center near Beit Shemesh. Rachael was just eight, and it was Gina who'd suggested we take the trip together, that we make a proper vacation of it, eagerly researching the country, updating our passports, and renting an apartment for the three of us just a few blocks from Gordon Beach. Set back on a quiet, tree-lined street in a handsome Bauhaus building, the bright and airy apartment on Rupin Street had proved a delightful surprise to us with its spare if tasteful furnishings, its sleek appliances, and its unobstructed view of the sea. Owned by French Jews, a Parisian couple with whom Gina had spoken on the telephone, the place was so comfortable, so convenient, that we'd quickly felt ourselves at home in that city by the sea, making a vow then and there to return the next year.

My father had been incensed by the idea of our going to Israel, for he'd hated what the country had become, what he'd viewed as the desecration of the Zionist dream by hawks and zealots like Shamir, Netanyahu, and Sharon. Angry, disillusioned, he'd derided the country for its militarism and hypocrisy, and for its rabid and intractable Haredim, those Ultra-Orthodox settlers now armed for redemption with their prayer books and guns.

Shortly after we'd made our plans to go, he and my mother had taken us to dinner at their favorite restaurant in New York, a little French place in midtown called Chez Napoleon, where, after a couple of drinks, he'd told us exactly how he felt. I remember he'd looked tired to me, and troubled, as if he and my mother had been fighting.

"Israel had a chance, you see, one chance," he'd told us, holding up a single blunt finger where we'd sat huddled together at a crowded little table near the bar. It had been snowing outside and I recall the scent of wet wool. "A chance to make something different, something better, something the world had never seen before—a secular, truly ethical dream of bricks and mortar designed and constructed by Jews!" He'd said this so loudly that for a moment the buzz in the restaurant had stopped. Impatient, my mother had tried to settle him, to change the subject, but he'd simply ignored her, gulping the last of his whiskey and looking around for the waiter, whom he'd signaled with impatience, shaking his glass at the man, before turning his attention to me.

For a moment my father had merely studied me from beneath his bushy black brows, bobbing his head like a fighter in a ring. At last he'd sat back and grinned, a taut, belligerent grin that had set me on guard.

"Does your daughter know what you do?" he'd demanded in a tone thick with menace.

"What do you mean, what I do?"

"Your job, David. Does she know how you make your money, how you pay for her dollies and clothes?"

"Of course she knows," Gina had snapped impatiently. She'd been on edge all night. "He tells her everything."

I was stunned. Gina defending me? For she'd never approved of my work, refusing to hear anything about it, even when I'd needed to speak of it, and punishing me with a silence that had all but crippled us that year. It was a measure of just how desperate she'd become.

As if sensing this, my father had grinned expediently, nodding his hoary head, only to reach across the table and pat Gina's hand, a signal—of warning, of reassurance—that he'd had no quarrel with her.

"Listen," I'd countered, feeling hot and claustrophobic. The wine had gone to my head and I was angry with him, angrier than I'd felt in years. "This isn't about me. It's about you, about what you think and believe. Everything you ever say and do is about you. Every article and book you write, every argument you provoke, every dinner table tirade you deliver is always and exclusively about you. Hell, you know nothing about my life, except the extent to which it has fallen short of your holy ideal for me. That's how it's always been, you hounding me day and night with your fucking yardsticks, never bothering, never once actually stopping to see who I am. Well take a look at me now," I'd commanded bitterly, thrusting my face across the table at him. "I am nothing like you!"

After that night, after we'd paid the bill and seen them to a taxi, I hadn't spoken with my father for nearly a year, though apparently he'd asked about me, now and then, about Gina and Rachael, about when we were planning to visit them in Ithaca again. He'd never inquired about our time in Israel, though my mother had told me that one day he'd sat for an hour with the photos of Israel that Gina had sent them, sipping a drink and nodding his head.

Most of the photos we'd copied for them were of Rachael—Rachael at the beach in Tel Aviv; Rachael at Masada; Rachael, head covered like a babushka, standing beside her mother at the Western Wall. Once when I was down here in Florida I'd found the photos among my father's things, shuffled together with an assortment of postcards and letters in a patched old banker's box, most of them faded with age. The bulk of the letters were from colleagues in the field, professional queries or commendations, though there were two from his father that had been franked in Paris at the Poste centrale du Louvre in '51 and '53 (which Post Office I'd visited one rainy afternoon, for no other reason than to stand where my grandfather had stood) and at least a half a dozen letters from my mother—mostly news and gossip—in her impeccable schoolgirl hand.

To my surprise I'd found stuck to the back of a drawing that Rachael had done in kindergarten a lone photograph of me taken in the Baha'i Gardens in Haifa that summer. The photo itself was unremarkable: posing awkwardly on the orange-graveled path before the Shrine of the Bab, I looked peevish, impatient, as if I'd had enough of touring that day, huffish and resentful to have been made to stand there in the broiling sun, though I can hardly remember our time in Haifa at all. What I do recall is that Rachael had been sick that day, sick with nausea and vomiting, and that Gina and I had quarreled for much of the train ride south along the coast. Now the photos are gone. Shortly after Rachael and I'd arrived yesterday, I'd looked for the box, hoping to set it aside for Rachael, only to find that my father had gotten rid of it, a fact he'd confirmed to me last night, with a devilish grin, clearly pleased to have outwitted me at last.

Now, looking at Rachael, I cannot help but feel sorry at the thought of that long and lazy summer in Israel, cannot help but recall it as the crowning experience of our life together as a family, a glowing, halcyon time that can never be repeated. We'd been happier there, in that land of ancient strife, than we'd ever been in New York, more trusting and generous with each other, more willing and able to forgive. We'd lived the time there openly, impulsively, swimming, reading, and napping by day, then feasting on kebabs and ice cream by night, when, arm-in-arm, we'd wandered the crowded tayelet, that sparkling promenade by the sea.

Through my job we'd made friends with a childless couple there, the Rosenzweigs, Chava and Benny. Chava was a senior architect with the Israeli firm that was overseeing the center I'd been hired to design; she'd met us at the airport the day we'd arrived in Israel and we'd quickly warmed to her brusque and impetuous charm. It was through her that we'd first gotten to know Tel Aviv, the parks and restaurants, the trendy Dizengoff with its shops and cafes, and the bustling Shuk Ha'Carmel where we'd gone once a week for our spices and food. One afternoon, shortly after we'd arrived, she'd taken us to Old Jaffa where we'd explored the narrow streets of the old Arab village, then watched the sunset from the terrace of a popular restaurant she knew called Aladin. In a jewelry shop there in Jaffa, one of many amidst the colorful galleries and cafes, I'd bought Gina an expensive Yemeni silver necklace, a gift so extravagant, so delightfully unlike her, she'd claimed, where we'd sat together over coffee at a crowded corner table that night, that she'd burst into tears.

Once back in New York our old habits had reasserted themselves with a vengeance, as if in retaliation for our absence that summer, so that soon I was travelling again, Gina was caught up in the demands of her new job at the Brooklyn Museum, and Rachael…why, we hardly saw Rachael at all, but now and then, when she'd emerge from her bubble of schoolwork and friends, apparently delighted by her life, to ask us for money or clothes. We did what New York families do. How were we to know?

Of course the signs had been everywhere apparent. We'd simply chosen to ignore them. And for a time it had worked. Then one night, Gina and I had gotten into an argument over how best to load the dishwasher, a clash so violent, so irrational, that for a moment we'd stood frozen there, too startled, too frightened to speak.

When finally Gina had broken the silence she'd looked at me, aghast.

"What has happened to you, David? I don't even know who you are."

"What are you talking about? So I hate the way you load the plates."

"You're not the man I knew." Head cocked, she'd said it in a whisper, as if just puzzling it out herself. "It's like some other man has taken your place."

"Don't be ridiculous. We're just tired. We're always tired. That's the problem. Every day the same damned thing and no chance to catch our breath. I mean, come on: I've got this new job in Atlanta and you…you're out the door every day before Rachael's even showered."

"So it's about my job, is it? Is that what you think?"

"No…I mean, yes. Of course it's about your job. It's about your job and its about my job. It's about everything at once!"

"You bastard," she'd hissed. "You know damned well it's not about my job. My job! Who do you think's been raising your daughter all these years, while you've been off chasing your fucking ego all over the world? That's right: me. Ever since you joined that firm, I've been living like a single mother here, taking care of Rachael and working full-time.

Do you know that she's failing math again? No, of course you don't. You have no idea that she's been getting in trouble with the nuns, do you, that last week I caught her throwing up her food? Have you even noticed her teeth?"

"Her teeth?"

"Yes, her teeth. Apparently she's been throwing up for months. That's what the counselor says. Months, David, and you hadn't the slightest idea!"

"Yes, but neither had you, and you've been with her every day. Gina, you have to understand, I'm not making excuses for myself. I should have been here, you're right. I should have been here to help. And still we might have missed it."

"So it has nothing to do with us? Is that what you're saying, David? Nothing to do with the fact that you're rarely home anymore, that when you are we always argue, that I have so much to do in a day that I haven't the time or the patience to sit with my own daughter and talk? Do you see what has happened to us, David? This is what I mean. She's crying for help and all you can do is catch the next flight out. Just look! You've already packed your bags," she'd exclaimed, pointing to my suitcase in the hall. "I tell you, I simply can't take this anymore."

"Listen. Listen to me," I'd implored her, holding her firmly by the shoulders in an effort to calm her. "I'll be back on Monday and we can talk about it again. I promise. We'll talk about it when we're calmer and we'll come up with a plan. A good plan. Something that'll really work. I swear," I'd pressed her, but she'd only shaken her head.

"You're never going to change, are you? Even now when it's almost too late. You still don't get it, do you?"

"Get what, Gina? That I've been neglectful, that I've lost perspective, that my priorities are all screwed up? I get it. Believe me. I get it all, but it's not enough just to see it, to say it out loud. I've explained this to you before. I've got deadlines, responsibilities. We've got bills to pay, remember? I can't simply do as I choose."

"Well, you're choosing now," she'd replied, coldly, freeing herself from my grasp and slowly, methodically tucking her hair behind her ears. The teapot had started whistling and she'd stared at it a moment before switching off the flame. "You remind me of your father, David. You always have, though I used to think you were different, too. Different in the ways that mattered most. Your father. He's the root of it, you know: your ambition, your anger, your fear. It seems like everything you do is in answer to him. Every squabble with me, every phone call, every conversation, its like you're talking to him. Even now he's here with us, isn't he? Yes, I can see it in your eyes; even now you're speaking to *him*."

"For God's sake, Gina, this has nothing to do with my father. Why does it always have to be about him?"

"Because it always is. Sooner or later, you're going to have to realize this, David. You're going to have forgive him— whatever he's done. You'll never rest until you do."

I watch now as the old fisherman takes in his line and assembles his things to go, saying something to Rachael that makes her throw back her head in laughter. As a parting gesture he offers her a fish, which he wraps in a page of newspaper for her. She has never liked fish, but accepts the gift anyway, thanking the man with a smile before joining me by the shop.

"He gave me a fish!" she exclaims, at once proud and appalled, handing me the soggy package and starting back toward the beach, to the restrooms to wash her hands. While I wait out front for her, I watch the old man as he trundles his way after us along the empty pier, rods and tackle in hand, then up the steep steps to the parking lot where he's parked his green truck. Only when he has started the engine and backed out of his parking space do I toss the fish in the trash.

At a shop on the beach near our car I buy Rachael a soda and a pink Ft. Myers sweatshirt, which she clutches happily to her chest for the short ride back.

Turning off at the exit for Punta Rassa, just before the island causeway, I suddenly regret having sold the Mercedes, for I've really enjoyed it today.

My mother had driven it everywhere with the top down, a colored scarf about her neck, speeding along the sea like Grace Kelly wending her way through the hills of Monaco. Before the Mercedes she'd never driven anything but an old blue Pontiac and a sputtering Volkswagen Bug, which had been riddled with nicks and dents and had filled up with fumes whenever the heater was switched on, so that even in the coldest weather she'd had to crack a window to save us from certain death.

Once we're back in the garage I take the time to search the car for anything my mother might have left inside it, knowing it is the last chance I'll have. I check the glove compartment, feel beneath the seats, and examine the various nooks and receptacles in the trunk, and am tempted to lift up the matting to examine the wheel-well beneath it, when behind me Rachael sighs. She is impatient for a swim, so that I'm forced to cut short my inspection, but not before bidding the old car farewell, which I do, patting its polished hood.

The moment we emerge from the elevator I know that something is wrong. The door of my father's apartment is ajar, the television blaring, the neighbor's cat seated complacently just inside. Shooing away the old tom, I hurry through the kitchen without setting down my things to find that my father is gone. To be certain I check his bedroom and the bathroom on the hall before switching off the television, the manic banter of which suddenly fills me with dread. I picture him crumpled at the bottom of the stairwell, see him floating face down in the pool, an image so stark, so horrid, that I rush to the window to check but the pool below is empty.

"Damn you!" I curse him before I can catch myself, though Rachael is not behind me. She is still in the hallway outside, talking to the neighbor, Mrs. Katz.

"Mrs. Katz, have you seen him?" I demand, pressing my face to the crack in her door, which she had opened to talk to Rachael, so that all I can see of her are her large, bulging eyes. She has the security chain in place and for an instant I feel the urge to kick in the door, to batter it down and drag her outside. "Have you seen my father go by?"

"No, no!" she squeaks fearfully and tries to close the door, but I stop it with my foot.

"Please, Mrs. Katz. This is serious. He could be anywhere by now."

"I told you I haven't seen him. I was sound asleep in my

bed. It's my head, you see…" she begins to protest, but I haven't the patience to listen to her complaints and dash to the elevator with Rachael in tow.

"Where do you think he's gone?" she asks me, once the door has closed. Impatiently I jab the buttons until at last, with a whine and a shudder, we begin our short descent. My mouth is dry; I feel nauseous from the heat.

"I don't know," I snap at her. "I really don't know. He could be at the marina, down by the ponds, anywhere. Hell, for all I know, he could be on a bus to Miami right now."

"But think. Where's he most likely to be?"

"Well, the marina, like I said. Then there's the pro shop where he had some friends. And the club. The club! Yes, he used to like to sit at the little bar there and have a drink before dinner. Do me a favor and check it out. In the meantime, I'll search the marina. Someone's bound to have seen him."

I am so preoccupied with the thought of my father, and with feeling sorry for myself, that the moment the door opens I collide with a woman trying to enter the car.

"David?" she says, stepping back to collect herself.

"Melina, hi! What are you doing here?" I can hardly believe my eyes.

"Clearing out my mother's place. She died last week. She'd been very sick."

"I'm terribly sorry. I had no idea."

"No, of course not. Anyway, it was a long time coming. What's wrong?" she demands, searching our faces.

"My father, he's gone."

"Gone? Gone where?"

"I've no idea. Rachael and I are…Sorry, Melina, this is my daughter Rachael. She's been helping me out."

"Hi there," says Melina, taking Rachael's hand, when, turning to me she says, "Come on, I'll help you look. He's bound to be close by."

"Yes, yes. Thanks. We could use another set of eyes," I stammer, uncomfortable under my daughter's steady gaze, and dismiss her with a kiss on the head. "Honey, why don't you head off to the clubhouse while Melina and I check with the manager at the marina. Call me on my cell the moment you learn something. Then we'll meet you back here."

Melina leads the way to the marina where my father kept his boat. Only slowly does it dawn on me that she is actually here, in the flesh. For her sudden appearance has flustered me, so that—sweaty, unshaven, feeling slack and heavy as I do—I hardly know what to think, to say, my tongue swollen, my pulse throbbing at the play of her slender hips as she negotiates her way down the path in her high-heeled shoes. She walks quickly so that by the time we reach the manager's office I am puffing for breath.

We find the assistant manager on duty, a pimply teenager in a Hawaiian print shirt, who tells us, leading us out along the dock, that virtually every man he sees here fits the description I've just given him. "All I can tell you is that there are a couple of old guys down that way," he directs us, indicating the far end of the marina, the end where my father had his slip.

The first man we find tinkering with the outboard motor of his dinghy; gruff, impatient with us, he replies that he hasn't seen anyone who matches the description of my father and promptly returns to his work. The other man, just a few slips down, is busy checking the rigging of his freshly painted sloop, and gladly welcomes us aboard, though Melina declines his offer, indicating her shoes. He is about my father's age, perhaps a little younger, with deeply burnished skin and a shock of stiff white hair. "We're looking for someone," I tell him. "A man about your height, if a bit stooped now. A little gray around the temples. We think he might have wandered down here to look at the boats."

"A sailor, eh?"

"Yes, well he used to be. Sold his boat a couple years back. Had a slip right over there. Perhaps you knew him...."

"Afraid not. Just moved down here from Richmond. I'll tell you what, though," he says, stepping nimbly off his boat. "Seems to me I saw a man like that last week when I was here registering my boat. Yeah, sat right over on that bench there, wearing nothing but shorts and a bathrobe. Pair a slippers on his feet." He shakes his head. "Looked like the world had gotten the best of him. Maybe twice. A real sorry lookin' fella, if you know what I mean."

"Well, listen, thank you," I tell him. "Do me a favor. If you see him again just let the manager know. He'll have my name and number."

On our way back to the office Melina suggests we check the boats at the other end of the marina, power boats mostly, the large gaudy cruisers for which my father had had nothing but contempt. He'd hated their imposition on the place, lamenting the fact so often to my mother that she'd taken to teasing him about it, remarking, whenever he'd complained, that she'd wished she'd married a man with a real boat, a luxury yacht with a hot tub, air conditioning, and satellite TV. On the sole occasion when they'd actually been invited aboard one of the yachts, an Italian-built cruiser, by friends of a friend, my father had spent the whole evening sulking on the aft deck with his glass of bourbon, where he'd remained even after their dinner was served. Unfortunately, there is no sign of him at this end of the marina and we are about to return, to meet up with Rachael at the apartment, when I spot him in his dark blue bathrobe, huddled behind the mizzen of a small wooden ketch.

His eyes are glassy, impassive, and at first he doesn't recognize me as I help him to his feet. He's convinced that the ketch is his, so that it is only by agreeing with him, by telling him that the manager would like a word with him before he sails, that I am able to lead him off the boat and back to the apartment, where, with Melina's help, I settle him in his chair.

"Poor man, he looks exhausted," she says, buttoning his pajama top and smoothing back his hair, though he reeks of urine. His breathing is fitful, shallow; suddenly he gulps at the air. "When's the last time he ate something?"

"I'm…I'm really not sure," I reply, embarrassed, the question clearly a reproof, which I accept without comment, following her into the little kitchen where she rummages around in the cupboards then checks the refrigerator. "I made him some cereal first thing this morning but he only knocked it to the floor."

"David, there's nothing in here!" she exclaims, holding the door ajar. "He needs food! Real food. I mean, he may be old but he still has to eat."

"I know," I protest feebly. "It's just that tonight's his last night here. We're taking him to a home tomorrow morning. A place over in Cape Coral…"

"But, David…"

"I know, I know. I'll pop out to the store right now and get him something good."

"Like what?" she demands, arms akimbo. "A candy bar? A bag of chips? Forget it. Let me see what I can find." Abashed, I watch her as she searches through the pantry and then disappears across the hallway to her mother's apartment.

Rachael is nowhere in sight and I take a moment to sit with my father, who drowses fitfully in his chair. He mumbles something about the tide, then something in Russian, when suddenly he clutches my arm, digging my wrist with his nails.

"You're not gonna get away with it," he rasps, a dry, hideous whisper, made all the more dreadful by his acrid-smelling breath. "I hear everything, see everything you do, and you're not gonna get away with it this time."

"Get away with what?" I reply as calmly I can, though he has caught me off guard. Even as I adjust his pillows I can feel his eyes on me, scouring my face.

"You and your filthy corporate masters! I see it all," he declares, "your swindles, your schemes. But you can't say I didn't warn you, David," he adds with an admonitory wag of his finger, when his eyes blaze wide: "Your sister saw it. Your mother saw it. Auden saw it, too: *We would rather be ruined than changed. We would rather die in our beds…*" he declaims to me, the professor, when briefly he stumbles, stammering, shaking his head and scowling, only to finish,

"*We would rather die in our beds than climb the cross of the moment!* Don't you see? We did our best to warn you, David, but who can reach you now? Who can penetrate that fortress you've made?"

"What fortress?"

"Surely not your friends," he blusters on, "those bankers and brokers, those plutocrats and CEOs who line their nests with our skins, our souls. No. I'm afraid that even they can't help you now."

"And you can?" I snort, struggling to get my bearings with him, for clearly his dementia has worsened, his delusions more paranoid, extreme, and still I cannot resist the urge to reply to him in kind. "You, with your ivory tower dictums? For God's sake, Dad, you've lived your whole life on a cozy college campus. What could you possibly know about the world out there?" I badger him, feeling flushed about the face and neck, a seemingly mild rebuke that somehow finds its mark, for suddenly his body stiffens, his features knotted with feeling. The change in him is alarming, his fists clenched tightly, his lips drawn blue against his teeth. But then, just as quickly, it passes; he shakes his head and grins.

"What, Dad?" I say. "What is it?" For now he snickers like a child, his head tucked turtle-like between his bony shoulders.

"It's true," he whispers. "I was waiting for him with a shovel that night! There in the rain by the shed."

"What night? What shovel?"

"Then you don't remember?" he says, cocking a weedy eyebrow at me.

"Remember what?" I snap, for I have no idea what he is talking about.

"You know, the little game you used to play with your mother's friend, Michael?"

"Michael? You mean, Michael Radetsky?" I reply, surprised, as though I hadn't thought of the man in years.

"Yes, Radetsky. Surely you remember the game."

"No," I say, anxiously, trying hard to recall it, to beat him to the punch, but my mind is blank. "Why, I hardly knew him at all."

"Is that so? Well then, let me see if I can jog your memory." He looks hard at me, nodding his head, when after a dismal pause in which I nearly rise to my feet he says, "Picture this: the four of us sitting out back of the house in Ithaca—you, your mother and Michael, and me. Its evening, late summer, the bats are out. I see wine on the table, hear one of your sister's records from a window upstairs. Michael has come to chat about his book, a little snag he can't untangle. He winks at you across the table and smiles… Now what was the name of that little game of yours?" he mutters theatrically, as if to himself, when his eyes flare cruelly. "That's right! Now I remember it. It was called 'What Then, Wherefore, Why'. Such a clever name, I'm amazed I forgot it. And you, only a boy of thirteen!"

"That? Come on," I say, rising abruptly from my chair. "It was just a silly little game, like counting the number of times a speaker says 'um'. We meant no harm by it."

"A silly little game? Is that all it was, a silly little game?"

"Yes, a silly little game. We were just teasing you a bit, that's all."

"And when you sat watch for your mother and Michael? Was that also a silly little game?"

"What are you talking about?"

"What am I talking about? he says." The question makes him chuckle, when he looks about him for his cigarettes, which he finds, after some searching, in the pocket of his robe. "Who knows? After all, maybe I have gone mad."

Of course his charge is outrageous. "I never sat watch for them," I reply hotly, though my voice quivers, a pitch too high, so that I feel the little boy again, standing helpless by his desk. "I was child, for God's sake. How can you possibly blame me?"

"Blame? What blame?" he replies blandly, scratching his stubbly chin. I watch him draw hard on the cigarette then exhale the smoke as he speaks. "I'm just curious, is all. Before you wash your hands of me tomorrow I'd simply like to know. Call it the peccadillo of a dotty old man."

"Well there's nothing to know." I am so angry I have to retreat to the window behind him to calm my trembling hands. "God, you make it sound like a conspiracy! You're like a cat with a mouse. Well, I'm not going to play your ugly little games today. I've played them all my life, and if I've learned anything in my forty-eight years of living it's that you never, ever play fair."

For a moment he is silent, no doubt parsing my words, when, after a lengthy pause in which it seems he has lost his focus again, he says, "I was talking with my sister the other day. Got a new dog, you know, some nasty little thing. I could hear it yipping in the yard. She was telling me about the little job you're working on out west there? Arizona, I think."

"New Mexico," I correct him before I can stop myself. For he's changed his tack again, so that I'm forced to follow him with care. To steady my hands I take up one of my mother's shells from the chest beneath the window, the large banded tulip she'd found on Turner Beach one morning after a particularly violent storm. I'm surprised to find it warm to the touch.

"Little job?" he chuckles. "Did I say 'little'? Forgive me. Your auntie tells me it's to be the largest of its kind in the world. Another first for America! Congratulations, David. You must be ever so pleased."

He is baiting me again, more like reeling me in, for we both know that he hooked me long ago. Though I'm tempted just to walk away, to finish up the packing in his study, to let him choke on his bile, I cannot resist the urge to face him now, to finally lay this struggle to rest.

Rubbing his chest he says, "What are they called again— maxi-maxis, MCM's?"

"That's good, Dad," I reply softly, evenly, for this time he will not get the best of me. "So you've done a little research. Good for you, though it's actually MCC's not MCM's. They're called Maximum Control Complexes, a fact I gladly would have shared with you if only you'd asked."

"No, don't be silly. You're a busy man, David. I wouldn't have wanted to trouble you, what with my being so witless, so old. In any case, what could you have said?"

"Why, I could have told you lots of things," I reply calmly, insouciantly. "Like what I do for my work—the busy meetings and late night hours, the trips around the world. I could have told you how successful I am, how respected in the field, shown you interviews and articles in glossy trade magazines. I could have shared with you the fact that out of more than a dozen national and international bids for this latest job it was mine alone that won. Had you asked I would have told you this, Dad, would have described for you my award-winning, my revolutionary designs. I would have told you all of this and more."

"Oh, if only I'd asked," he mocks me, raising the footrest of his chair and sighing gravely. "If only I'd asked I would have seen the real you, David, would have recognized you for the genius you are." Malevolently he grins. "If only I'd asked I might have bragged about you to my friends at the club. 'David? Oh, yes, David's doing splendidly. Right now he's hard at work on a project out in New Mexico that is to change the very nature of incarceration as we know it. Instead of those outdated, inefficient old prisons designed for the reformation of convicts, designed," he adds with a snicker, "after the preposterous belief that human beings can change, that deep down there is something good in them, all of them, something worthy of hope, the prisons of today are being fashioned with a very different objective in mind. Incapacitation, I think they call it—and all at a tidy profit!

"Understand," he adds quickly, before I can interrupt him. "I'm hardly an expert on the matter, but I can tell you this," he whispers behind his hand at me, as if still in conference with one of his fellow sailors at the club. "I can tell you that it bodes well for the likes of us. For people like you and me. All those niggers and spics! If only we could find way to get the chinks and a-rabs, too..."

"Are you finished?" I say. "Because, if you are, I've got a

tip for you, Dad. If you don't like the way the system works then tell your damned congressman about it. Not me. The uses and abuses of prisons are not my business. All I do is design them. What happens inside them has nothing to do with me."

"Just following orders then, eh?"

I am about to reply when I hear the front door open, followed by the click of Melina's heels on the kitchen tiles. She has returned with my father's food, which she sets on the counter without a word before returning across the hall. "Listen," I counter bitterly, once she's gone, hissing the words through my teeth, "nobody tells me what to do. The only orders I follow are my own. I make a bid for a job and, more often than not, I get it. I get it because I'm good. Give me the budget and specs and there's nothing I can't do."

"*Won't* do, you mean. There's nothing you won't do, if the price is right. I've seen your Guantanamo, your Abu Ghraib. You'll design your black sites and death camps for anyone with enough money, gulags and ghettos for all the world's poor. But none of that compares with this, this latest project of yours. No. Nothing you've ever done is half so cynical as this. Why, it's worthy of the great Piranesi himself!" he exclaims, cackling brightly. "Such a fiendish eye you have for human suffering, David. It's a wonder I never saw it before. I mean, a spiral, a labyrinth! Who but you could have imagined such a thing?"

"Listen, my firm had nothing to do with Abu Ghraib. And it was Halliburton that built Guantanamo. I was just a consultant."

"Just a consultant! You mean like Goebbels?"

"Bravo, Dad. There it is! I knew it was only a matter of time before you found your way home again." And still I shake my head. "Goebbels! You're actually comparing me to Goebbels? Did it ever occur to you that maybe prisons are a good thing, that, for all their flaws, we're actually better, safer for them? Yes, I know, I know," I say, before he can reply. "I know what you believe, Dad—that people are basically good inside, that, given the right circumstances, that is, freed from ignorance and poverty and provided with reasonable healthcare and education, they'd more than likely make the right choices and we'd all live happily ever after. I've heard that record all my life and, you know, and it's finally starting to skip. Hell, the fucking needle's jumped clear out of the groove!" I hector him, glancing out the window to collect myself, when I'm arrested by my father's coughing, his body convulsing so violently I fear he'll tumble from his chair.

Yet even before I can reach him the paroxysm passes. Head back, lungs heaving, he has closed his eyes, and for a moment I study his wasted face. His skin, faintly jaundiced, glistens with sweat, his hair stuck in strands to his long and mottled skull. He gabbles madly and, though I lower my ear to his lips, I cannot grasp what he says.

"Dad, Dad, are you alright?" I demand, making no attempt to hide my alarm, even squatting beside his chair to get a better look at him, when he startles me with a snort.

"Fool! Look at you. You've got your head so far up your ass you don't know if its night or day. You couldn't possibly believe that these prisons you're designing have anything to do with justice. With keeping us safe in our beds. No, no," he chuckles wryly, "you're much too smart for that. It's merely something you've taught yourself to say. Isn't that right? And no wonder. Serving a god like yours, how else could you look your daughter in the eye?"

"So now you recognize her, do you? I should have known that you've been playing us all along."

"Of course I recognize her. And I recognize you," he says coldly, fixing me with his pale blue eyes. "You see, I know why you're here, David."

"Do you now?" I scoff at him, briefly turning to break his gaze.

"Yes, I do. You've come to beg my forgiveness. Isn't that right? To secure my blessing before you lock me away."

"Forgiveness! Forgiveness for what? For my life, my job? I'm proud of what I do. And as for locking you away, you know perfectly well that you can no longer manage on your own. Just look at this place!"

"Proud," he repeats distractedly, when he fixes his eyes on me. I refuse to look away. "Yes, you should be very proud of yourself, David—the isolation, the depravation, the systematic destruction of self. Imagine: twenty-three hours a day, every day, confined to a 6' x 8' cell in which your every breathing moment is monitored by closed-circuit TV, a windowless cage of poured concrete and steel in which the florescent lights are never, ever switched off. Amazing, really. The loneliness, the babbling. The jerking off in plain sight. Why, you've even soundproofed the cells, poor shmucks— not even the dignity of their own screams!"

Trembling, I am about to rebut him, to cut him to the quick at last, when he lifts a hand to stop me. Briefly, he has hunched forward in the chair as if in preparation for another fit of coughing, yet he doesn't cough this time, wheezing anxiously instead. "No, you're not going to get away with it," he gasps, settling back in the chair, his eyes pinched in pain. "I've taken measures this time and you're not going to get away with it."

"Get away with it! What are you talking about? Get away with what, Dad? Your money? You don't have a fucking penny to your name! You never have. Get away with it? I don't want to get away with anything!" I despair aloud to him, for he has clearly lost his focus again, lips fluttering, fingers wriggling uselessly in his lap like a pair of upturned crabs. He mutters drunkenly, waving at the air, and just when I'm about to shake him, to force him to look at me, he starts in his chair, eyes wide with terror, only to moisten his lips and sigh, addressing me finally, where I stand beside him, with a wan and anguished grin.

"I was thinking of my father this morning," he says at length, smiling wryly at his fingertips. His tone is gentle, rapt. "You never really knew him, David. A shame, really. Such a pity his life."

"Why a pity?" I begrudge him, for once again he has switched the subject, seized the upper hand before I can speak my mind.

"A pity because he failed, all his efforts for naught. That's the pity. He got trapped by his own zeal, he hated the Nazis so much. Painted himself into a corner and the world will never forgive him that."

"You mean his defense of Stalin?"

"He got trapped, your grandfather. Forced to defend the

indefensible. And for that there is no forgiveness." Grimly he shakes his head. "History is stingy that way, devouring a million men a day only to spit up the bones of but two or three. The American Communist Party! An oxymoron, a joke. Such, says the consensus, was your grandfather's life—a sham, a disgrace. 'A clique of dreary fanatics'! That's what Schlesinger called them. 'Sodden, contentious, and feeble.' But know this, David: your grandfather was anything but feeble." Painfully now he grins. "Don't you see, he died hoping—and that, my boy, is something. For all his dogma, for all his vanity and pride, there was nothing cynical about him. Hell, he believed in *me*! That's the way he was. He had a trust in human nature the like of which seems impossible, derisible today, a nearly messianic faith in the goodness of people, in their potential, that defied all reason, that defied plain common sense. And oh how I despised him for it! You have no idea," he cavils bitterly, finding a crumpled cigarette and raising it to his lips.

"Don't you see?" he cries, rapping his skull so hard with his knuckles that I'm tempted to stop him. "He *knew*, your grandfather, deep down he knew that a life without hope was hardly worth living. He simply refused to turn bitter, no matter how they humiliated him, no matter how they knocked him down," he exclaims, eyes agog, when briefly he winces, his face a sickly, ashen gray. His chest is heaving and I try to settle him, to help him catch his breath, but he repels me with a force that nearly knocks me off my feet. "Hope, David!" he bellows at me. "He refused to give up hope. And believe me when I tell you that there is nothing harder to sustain in this life than hope. Hatred and violence and fear of God, why, they're nothing compared to what it takes just to smile each day. Look around you, boy!" he cries, shaking the daily paper at me. "The proof is everywhere you turn—the lying and spying, the torture, belligerence, and greed. And the worse part, the worse part, David, is that when I look at you now, when I think of your life, of your precious little girl, all I can do is weep…"

He has pushed me too far. "Am I really such a disappointment to you?" I demand, as disgusted as I am amazed, for his eyes are actually wet. "What, you think I have no feeling at all? That all I care about is money? I don't give a damn about money! That's how little you know me, Dad. Yet I shouldn't be surprised: you've never bothered to know me at all. It's true! You've always seen me as a child. High school, college, even when I was married and making my way in the world, I was always the same to you, the same cringing little boy you used to badger on the field when I missed a pitch or dropped a fly ball. And for what—and why? Why all those years of heckling and derision when you never really had an interest in me to begin with, so caught up in your petty academic skirmishes that you couldn't see the forest for the trees. Me, Mom…hell, you couldn't see poor Lily at all! But who I am to judge you? Who am I to care? The truth is, I've no wish to convince you of anything anymore."

I am about to go, to find Rachael, when turning abruptly I add, "It's funny, the night before I flew down here, you know what I was hoping, Dad? I was hoping I'd find you dead. I was hoping I'd find you dead in your chair there, so that all I'd have to do is get an ambulance to come and cart you away. But here you are, alive and well, well alive anyway, and nothing, not a single damned thing has changed.

"That's the heart of it, Dad: nothing ever changes with you. Once you've reached a verdict on someone or something, once you've made your appraisal, there's no shaking it, no matter how I've grown or changed. And, yes, I'm talking about me—about my job, my marriage, my life. You've never forgiven me anything, never talked to me, never even tried to understand. I mean, for God's sake, do you actually think I chose to design prisons, that I derive some sick sort of pleasure from it? Do you think I wanted my marriage to fail? And what about Rachael?" I despair aloud to him, so that the blood hammers in my brain. "My own daughter… Why, I hardly know Rachael at all!

"But you, you think it's all so easy, that a man's life is nothing but a series of simple choices, that he can pick and choose as he pleases. Well, the world doesn't work that way, Dad. It never has and never will.

"Still, you're right about me; you've been right all along. I made a deal with the devil and the price I've paid is dear. You're right about that, Dad—and wrong. I didn't choose to design prisons; I chose to be an architect. I chose the world out there," I exclaim, pointing at the bridge, the bay. "That big messy world with all its lying and hypocrisy, with all its bigotry, indifference, and pain. Don't you see? I had to face it, I had to get away. Surely you understand this, Dad, that I didn't…that I didn't want to end up like you."

For a moment I study his anguished face, but it is impossible to tell what if anything he's grasped. And suddenly I see myself in his chair, some decades hence, the hollowed eyes and cheeks, the twitching lips, the penis (exposed where he sits) a pied and shriveled fig. I see myself alone, see the room, the TV, smell the urine and vomit and shit, and try to shake the monstrous image, even rising to my feet, when my father whimpers, a strange, disquieting sound that tightens my stomach, my groin.

"Do…do you remember what I told you?" he stammers in a voice cracked with feeling. It is a voice I've never heard before. Even the look on his face is strange: there is a softness in his eyes, a nakedness that makes me think that death is gentle, too, even bashful, expectant, afraid.

"No," I say. "What did you tell me, Dad?"

"Something my father told me, when I was a boy just starting the seventh grade. We lived in Brooklyn then, you remember? On St. John's Place. Do you remember the building?"

"In Brooklyn there, yes. I remember the street."

"Yes, the street…" he murmurs, shaking his hoary head. "He was very strict, my father, no to this and no to that, always throwing his weight around like he had nowhere else to go, for it was really my mother who was in charge of things. It was her house, her mother's house, no matter how my father shouted, no matter what he claimed. He could scream all he liked; my mother didn't care. When she was angry with him she left his dinner in the oven until it burned. Yet my father, too, was proud. I can see him at the little table in the kitchen there, after a long day at work, napkin tucked fast in his collar, chewing the blackened bits like he was seated in a fine French restaurant, enjoying filet mignon. One night he said to me, 'Jackie, (he had eaten his dinner alone and I remember the bourbon on his breath), he said to me, 'Jackie, whatever you do with your life, make sure that you can sleep at night. You hear me, boy? There is nothing more precious than sleep.'"

"Yes, I remember it!" I cry, eager as I am to believe it, to keep my father engaged, for again he has closed his eyes and I fear that he is dying.

There is so much I wish to tell him, so much I wish to say, but I cannot rouse him now and nearly cry out for help, when he groans aloud. He shudders, frowns, then grins at nothing. I feel a tension in my throat, and suddenly the words come pouring out: "Dad, I'm sorry," I exclaim. "Do you hear me, Dad? I'm different now; I am. I know what you mean." But he doesn't respond, wheezing faintly where he sits, and still I cannot stop myself, cannot stem the words that rush from lips. "You've got to believe me, Dad. I know that something has to give; if only for Rachael's sake I've got to make a change. I know that. I promise you, Dad, I will."

My heart is racing; I can barely steady my hands, and suddenly I'm crouching by his chair. "Dad, Dad," I press him, aghast, amazed, hardly knowing what it is I want from him, what it is I long to say. "There's a story I tried to tell you the last time I was here." He looks at me, bewildered by emotion, eyes shining, lips quivering with grief, and it's clear he's fading fast. In a matter of minutes he may not know me at all.

Desperate I squeeze his arm. "Do you remember I told you about that boy? The one out in the middle of the desert there, this little Mexican boy in brown pants and a ratty blue shirt? He was sick from the sun and the heat—he'd been walking for miles—and I sat with him in the air-conditioned cab of the foreman's truck, stroking his head and talking aloud to him about anything and everything, singing jingles and nursery rhymes, singing anything I could think of to keep him conscious, to keep him awake, because his eyes kept closing on me, Dad, until he couldn't open them anymore and I knew that he was dead...

"Dad, Dad," I implore him, for suddenly his eyes have gone blind, his lips abruptly, alarmingly still. "The little boy was dead! They took him away by helicopter and for days I sat alone in my hotel room, staring out over the border where the city creeps like smog, and not even the foreman could reach me.

"Then...then it was the oddest thing," I explain, as much to myself as to him, feeling the same strange lightness in my chest. "I woke one morning and it was gone. I showered and dressed and was back on the job and no one said a word to me. A week or so later the Border Patrol found the boy's father face-down in a ditch about half a dozen miles from the site." I say it softly, indifferently, for I know that I've lost him, my father, that perhaps forever this time I have vanished in his eyes. Indeed he seems but dimly aware that I've been speaking to him at all, studying my face with that vacant fascination I've seen before. And still I cannot stop myself, clutching his bony hands and insisting: "Dad, the boy and his father had trekked for miles across the desert— and for what? A prison! A fucking prison! Do you hear me? Please, just smile or nod. Just squeeze my hand if you do," I beg him vainly, for he only stares at me, his fingers limp in my grip.

Shaken, uncertain what to do, I am about to rise when I see that he is crying. He is looking straight at me and crying, and it seems that the whole world has gone still, so numb, so muddled do I feel, when he squeezes my hand and sighs.

It is everything, enough: Mrs. Katz is listening to the radio on her terrace next door, a lawnmower hums, I hear Rachael at the door, and quickly kiss my father on the head, turning up the volume on the television until he looks at the screen.

On the kitchen table I find the meal that Melina has prepared for him—some fruit cocktail, a slice of whole wheat toast, and a bowl of macaroni and cheese gone cold. Beside it she has folded a white cloth napkin the way that waiters in fine restaurants do. For some reason the gesture makes me think of my mother, though it is the not the sort of thing she'd have done.

I knock twice on Melina's door before she opens it and am struck at once by her beauty, so plain, so apparent now that I touch her face, her hair, which is damp at the temples; I kiss her gently on the lips. And she is not surprised, but considers me frankly and grins.

Dressed now in a faded green t-shirt and flower print skirt, she is clearing out her mother's kitchen drawers, the contents of which lie strewn across the brightly tiled countertop, her whisks and spatulas and spoons.

"Did he eat?" Melina asks me, reaching to the back of one of the narrow drawers, which appears to have gotten stuck.

"No, but thanks. He's dozing again. I'll try again later."

"So how'd it go?" she says.

Weary, elated, I smile. "Hard to say, really. With my father it's always hard to say."

She has taken down the heavy curtains in the living room, the dark Spanish furniture, somber paintings, and Lladró figurines now garish in the pale and watery light.

"What will you do with your mother's things?" I ask her, pulling out one of the stools at the counter. She has set aside one of her mother's cookbooks, a cookbook in Spanish, I see, and briefly I flip through the pages, pausing here and there to decipher the handwritten notes.

"I'll sell them, I guess. Or give them away. I've already taken the things I want," she explains without feeling, wiping out the inside of the drawer, when apropos of nothing she remarks, "She never really liked it here."

"Your mother? She always seemed happy to me."

"No. Every day she wanted to return to Cuba, but then my father died, and then her sister in Matanzas died, and there was no longer any reason to go. See that picture there?" she says, indicating a small framed photo at the end of the counter. "She grew up there, a little town called Santa Cruz del Norte. She often told me about it, about the fishermen and the beach, and about her father's job as foreman in the national distillery there. She loved her father more than anyone in the world and it broke her heart to leave him. By then he was pretty sick and she never saw him again. Of course my father blamed Castro for it, but my mother never blamed anyone but herself."

Taking up the murky photograph, she smiles enough to

say, "She never claimed the town was anything special. Parts of it were really quite ugly, she said, but she liked the smell of the fish and the way you could always hear the sea. Even with the radio on."

I look at the picture—at the palm tree, the storefronts, the wide, empty street, and try to think of something comforting to say, when she asks me, "What about your father? Do you think he's been happy here?"

The question puzzles me. It has been so long since I've thought of my father's happiness that I can only shake my head. "I have no idea, really. I mean I hope so. I hope he's been happier here. I know my mother was. I know at least he was happy for that."

"Do you know he once took me sailing?"

"My father? When?" I press her, for the notion is astounding.

"I don't know…the summer my father died? Your mother was off somewhere. I think it was June. He asked my mother to come along as well but she wasn't feeling up to it, so I went along by myself."

"And?"

"And nothing. We had a lovely sail. Up to Bokeelia and back," she explains haltingly, as if trying to recollect the details, when affectionately she smiles. "Did you know he was once afraid of the sea? Petrified. So scared, he told me, that he used to cry when his mother took him to the beach at Rockaway. She was always trying to get him to swim. That's why he joined the Navy, he said."

"No, he never told me that. What else did he say?"

"Not much really. For the most part we didn't talk at all,

just listened to the flapping of the sails," she explains, when, sensing my disappointment, she adds, "He's been very kind to me these past few months, checking in on me whenever I was here. He brought my mother some flowers one day. They were lilies, your mother's favorite, I think. He set them in a vase by her bed."

Self-consciously now, she tucks her hair behind her ears, fiddling for a moment with one of her earrings. "It's funny, the night of my mother's funeral I heard the television on inside your father's place and just let myself in without knocking. Of course he was happy to see me. He poured me a large bourbon and together we watched the ballgame until I fell asleep in the chair."

"I'm glad," I reply, for somehow it pleases me to think of the two of them together—the baseball and bourbon, the sea breeze and sunshine and sails. And suddenly I see how it ends, this visit, this day: I see my father and Rachael; I see Melina and Rachael and me.

"So you're taking him to Sanibel this evening?" she inquires at length, bending down to remove some of her mother's pots and pans from the cabinet by the stove.

"Sanibel?"

"Rachael told me you were thinking of taking your father for a walk by the water there."

"Yes. Yes, that's right. He and my mother used to drive over to the lighthouse after dinner to get an ice cream and stroll along the beach. It was Rachael's idea. You know, for old time's sake," I explain, thinking again of my mother, my father, when I realize that Melina is looking at me. Pot in hand, she is kneeling by the stove, when without a word

I lift her to her feet. Her lips part, her breath quickens; I fumble for the hem of her skirt.

Melina and Rachael get my father dressed and soon he is standing at the door, shoes tied, shirt buttoned to the neck, hair combed smoothly across his broad, freckled pate. Grinning with pleasure, he reminds me of a boy risen early for school.

Remarkably, he'd offered no resistance when Melina stripped him of his pajamas then bathed him with a warm wet cloth, even chuckling a bit when she wiped his penis and balls. She'd insisted on taking charge of his preparation, a task to which she has devoted herself with such patience, such care, that it is nearly seven by the time we reach the car.

I guide my father into the front seat of the Chrysler, reaching across his shrunken frame to fasten his seatbelt. Scrubbed clean, he smells freshly of soap. Melina and Rachael have settled themselves in the back, Rachael behind my father, Melina behind me, so that I can see her in the rearview mirror as I reverse the car.

It is a beautiful Florida evening, the sky beyond the causeway streaked with high white clouds. Even at this hour the bay is speckled with sailboats, the tiny causeway islands crowded with the cars and trucks of day fisherman reluctant to go home. The traffic flows smoothly and in minutes we are there, on Sanibel Island, where at the first stop sign I turn left on Periwinkle Way, following it down to the little row of shops before the entrance to Lighthouse Point.

At first my father is confused. "Where are we? What is this place?" he demands anxiously, perhaps thinking it's tomorrow, that we're taking him to The Villas, but then he recognizes the ice cream shop and clucks with joy. His order, two scoops of Dutch chocolate in a large sugar cone, is invariably the same, and I cannot help but envy him, as I guide him to the bench out front, the simple pleasure of each grave and focused lick.

The experience for him is transformative, like a link between selves, so that he chatters blithely while he eats, nimbly recalling happier times and giddily making jokes. Melina laughs with him, then Rachael, and his skinny chest swells with the attention.

No one else has gotten ice cream, so that once my father is finished, once I've wiped his hands and mouth, we drive the short distance to the point where we park the car in the lot by the beach. Fearing the walk along the water will be too much for him, we take the nature trail instead, a short wooden boardwalk that zigzags its way to the lighthouse through a dense cover of seagrape and mangroves.

Rachael has taken my father by the arm and leads him on ahead of us, pointing at this and that, talking volubly in her avid teenaged way, and suddenly I feel the weight of Time itself, thick as the air about us and nearly visible—there and there—in the light between the leaves. Beside me Melina is quiet, perhaps thinking of her mother, her father, perhaps wondering, like me, what it all should mean, this walk, this evening, this shimmering tunnel of green.

The two of us stop at the lighthouse to take off our shoes, so that by the time we reach the empty beach Rachael has removed my father's sandals, rolled up his pant legs, and led him out into the gently frothing surf. Hair flying in the breeze, he is singing a song, an aria by Donizetti or Puccini, snippets of which are carried across the shell-covered sand to where we stand amidst the sea-wrack and driftwood, generous as lovers, chary as husband and wife. The scene itself is mythical: the light, the sea. There young Nausikaa helps my father to shore.

Acknowledgements

First and foremost I would like to thank my mother, Dr. Linda Rennie Forcey, for her deeply-engaging 1979 study, *Personality in Politics: The Commitment of a Suicide,* the seed from which this story grew. Her support has been invaluable to me. I would like to thank my good friends and colleagues, George Ovitt and David Gutierrez, for their patience in reading drafts of this novel, and for their keen and abiding friendship. It is hard to imagine my days without them. Similarly, I would like to express my gratitude to my dear friends, Wallace Sheid and Audrey De Souza-Sheid, for their generous hospitality when I stayed with them in El Paso. My time with them there proved instrumental to this tale. Then I am grateful, deeply grateful, to Marc Estrin and Donna Bister of Fomite Press whose professionalism, politics, and bold literary vision are an inspiration to me. Finally, I would like to thank my wife, Annie Nash, for the extraordinary example that is her life. I would be lost without her.

Peter Nash is the author of a biography called *The Life and Times of Moses Jacob Ezekiel: American Sculptor, Arcadian Knight*. He has published poems and stories in *Desideratum, Berkeley Poetry Review, The Avalon Literary Review*, and *The Minetta Review*, and has recently completed a novel called *The Perfection of Things* about a failed biographer of the Austrian-Jewish author and suicide, Stefan Zweig. In 2012, he co-founded and now writes a bi-weekly post for a literary blog called *Talented Reader*: http://talentedreader.blogspot.com/. He lives in New Mexico with his wife and two sons.

About Fomite

A fomite is a medium capable of transmitting infectious organisms from one individual to another.

"The activity of art is based on the capacity of people to be infected by the feelings of others."
—Tolstoy, *What Is Art?*

Writing a review on Amazon, Good Reads, Shelfari, Library Thing or other social media sites for readers will help the progress of independent publishing. To submit a review, go to the book page on any of the sites and follow the links for reviews. Books from independent presses rely on reader to reader communications.

For more information or to order any of our books, visit
http://www.fomitepress.com/FOMITE/Our_Books.html

More Titles from Fomite...

Novels

Joshua Amses — *During This, Our Nadir*
Joshua Amses — *Raven or Crow*
Joshua Amses — *The Moment Before an Injury*
Jaysinh Birjepatel — *The Good Muslim of Jackson Heights*
Jaysinh Birjepatel — *Nothing Beside Remains*
David Brizer — *Victor Rand*
Paula Closson Buck — *Summer on the Cold War Planet*
Roger Coleman — *Skywreck Afternoons*
Marc Estrin — *Hyde*
Marc Estrin — *Kafka's Roach*

Marc Estrin — *Speckled Vanitie*
Zdravka Evtimova — *In the Town of Joy and Peace*
Zdravka Evtimova — *Sinfonia Bulgarica*
Daniel Forbes — *Derail This Train Wreck*
Greg Guma — *Dons of Time*
Richard Hawley — *The Three Lives of Jonathan Force*
Lamar Herrin — *Father Figure*
Ron Jacobs — *All the Sinners Saints*
Ron Jacobs — *Short Order Frame Up*
Ron Jacobs — *The Co-conspirator's Tale*
Scott Archer Jones — *A Rising Tide of People Swept Away*
Maggie Kast — *A Free Unsullied Land*
Darrell Kastin — *Shadowboxing with Bukowski*
Coleen Kearon — *Feminist on Fire*
Coleen Kearon — *#triggerwarning*
Jan Englis Leary — *Thicker Than Blood*
Diane Lefer — *Confessions of a Carnivore*
Rob Lenihan — *Born Speaking Lies*
Colin Mitchell — *Roadman*
Peter Nash — *Parsimony*
Ilan Mochari — *Zinsky the Obscure*
Gregory Papadoyiannis — *The Baby Jazz*
Andy Potok — *My Father's Keeper*
Robert Rosenberg — *Isles of the Blind*
Ron Savage — *Voyeur in Tangier*
David Schein — *The Adoption*
Fred Skolnik — *Rafi's World*
Lynn Sloan — *Principles of Navigation*
L.E. Smith — *The Consequence of Gesture*
L.E. Smith — *Travers' Inferno*
Bob Sommer — *A Great Fullness*
Tom Walker — *A Day in the Life*

Susan V. Weiss —*My God, What Have We Done?*
Peter M. Wheelwright — *As It Is On Earth*
Suzie Wizowaty — *The Return of Jason Green*

Poetry

Antonello Borra — *Alfabestiario*
Antonello Borra — *AlphaBetaBestiaro*
James Connolly — *Picking Up the Bodies*
Greg Delanty — *Loosestrife*
Mason Drukman — *Drawing on Life*
J. C. Ellefson — *Foreign Tales of Exemplum and Woe*
Anna Faktorovich — *Improvisational Arguments*
Barry Goldensohn — *Snake in the Spine, Wolf in the Heart*
Barry Goldensohn — *The Hundred Yard Dash Man*
Barry Goldensohn — *The Listener Aspires to the Condition of Music*
R. L. Green When — *You Remember Deir Yassin*
Kate Magill — *Roadworthy Creature, Roadworthy Craft*
Tony Magistrale — *Entanglements*
Sherry Olson — *Four-Way Stop*
Andreas Nolte — *Mascha: The Poems of Mascha Kaléko*
Janice Miller Potter — *Meanwell*
Joseph D. Reich — *Connecting the Dots to Shangrila*
Joseph D. Reich — *The Hole That Runs Through Utopia*
Joseph D. Reich — *The Housing Market*
Joseph D. Reich — *The Derivation of Cowboys and Indians*
Kennet Rosen and Richard Wilson — *Gomorrah*
Fred Rosnblum — *Vietnumb*
David Schein — *My Murder and Other Local News*
Scott T. Starbuck — *Industrial O*
Scott T. Starbuck — *Hawk on Wire*
Seth Steinzor — *Among the Lost*
Seth Steinzor — *To Join the Lost*

Stories

Odd Birds

Micheal Breiner — *the way none of this happened*
David Ross Gunn — *Cautionary Chronicles*
Gail Holst-Warhaft — *The Fall of Athens*
Roger Leboitz — *A Guide to the Western Slopes and the Outlying Area*
dug Nap— *Artsy Fartsy*
Delia Bell Robinson — *A Shirtwaist Story*
Peter Schumann — *Planet Kasper, Volumes One and Two*
Peter Schumann — *Bread & Sentences*
Peter Schumann — *Faust 3*
Peter Schumann — *We*

Plays

Stephen Goldberg — *Screwed and Other Plays*
Michele Markarian — *Unborn Children of America*

www.ingramcontent.com/pod-product-compliance
Lightning Source LLC
Chambersburg PA
CBHW050354190726
48284CB00007BB/2282